Hooked

Madilynn Dale

Copyright

Trigger Warning:
Mention of rape, death, fighting, cursing, addiction, ro-mance, hint at sex, attempted rape, alcohol, mild blood, magic, de-ception, captivity, kidnapping, pirates, plank walking, drunkenness.
Previously Published as Hooked on Kindle Vella
Cover by The Chapter Goddess LLC

Contents

the CHAPTER Goddess

Chapter 1

Glaring at the world around me, an old fisherman's saying floats through my mind. Red sky at night, sailors' delight. Red sky in the morning, sailors take warning. I wonder, does the saying apply to more? I wish I'd asked my father before he was killed. Would I have been prepared for this attack if I knew it applied to more than the weather? I guess it's too late now.

I hold my position and curse as my arm shakes, sweat pouring down my brow. I'm forced to sidestep and swing my sword up in an arc as my opponent lunges at me. Our weapons meet and we cross from one end of the deck to the other. The echo of metal striking against metal fills the air around us as we continue our deadly dance. Only one will survive, and I'll be damned if it's not me.

The wretched woman across from me smirks. I know she wants me gone, and to stop my ship, but I refuse. My father trained me against all types of opponents, and she's no different. Even with her background, I know, somehow, she can be defeated. The ancestral blood that fills her veins doesn't aid her. She's nothing without her cheating pixie dust. You take that away and I'm sure she wouldn't fare much against me and my sword.

I grimace, forcing myself to focus on my task. With screams

and groans filling the air, her crew fights a losing battle against mine. Why they bothered with us today is beyond me, but I won't back down without a fight.

The churning sea encourages me as I clench my jaw, it's as if it knows how volatile I am, and I focus on my movements. The salty spray splashes up the sides of the ship, coating the deck and creating another obstacle for my crew to face as the flying idiots attack. It takes skill to keep from slipping as we move, and thankfully that's something we've trained for.

Seeing an opening on my opponent's left, I swing my sword only for her to lift into the air and unleash a shrill bird call at the last second. The fighting stops around us as her crew takes to the air to escape, hooting and hollering like kids. My opponent cackles loudly as she flies higher toward the clouds, growing smaller the further she goes. Coward.

"That stupid Sparrow! I can't believe she did this to my ship! Why did she break from her usual pattern?" I glare at the skies as Norma Pan disappears into the clouds. Her dark grey and green clothing camouflages her against the stormy clouds. She's a menace and enjoys provoking us without reason, but today is different.

I glance around as I stand with my fist clenched at my side. The mast of my ship is lane over halfway into the dark waters of the Manica Sea. The dark wood turns colors as it soaks up water. Creaks and scuffles fill the air around me as my crew gathers those who were injured from the fight. The Sparrow managed to surprise us and I'm not sure how she did it.

I glance around, cursing under my breath, trying to determine how to make it to the nearest port. Which one was it? It couldn't have been too long ago we were at one. Was it the port at Alandra? Would we make it through the storm that's brewing?

"Captain James, I think we can manage to row to Ciara, the small island we passed not too long ago," my first mate Jody Lee says respectfully, reading my mind as usual. She appears out of the shadows with flecks of blood scattered along her tunic. Not a scratch mars her lean figure.

"Thank you. This was an unusual attack. I don't understand

why she came this far out and can't leave us alone! We don't bother her, and no one dares near the island she inhabits." I groan as I cross the deck toward my quarters.

My feet cause the boards beneath me to creak more than usual, and I can't help but wonder if the mast caused more damage than we originally thought when it fell over. Did it weaken the flooring of the deck? I glance down, expecting to see cracks, but none are present. It gives me a small relief.

Jody stays on my heels and drops her voice to a whisper as we approach my door. "Silver, you know why she harasses us. She blames you for her sister's disappearance. How dare Pan's descendants fall in love and run away with yours? Your father despised Pan, and he him."

I sigh and push open my door. Stupid blood feud. It should have ended when my father did. Jody closes the door behind her with a loud thud and I glance at my desk across the room. Papers cover it and a small wooden cup holds feathered pens. A few ink wells rest next to it.

"I get that, but they were happy. That's why I helped them get off this planet. It also let us squander goods from all those ships near the dock. With those magical portals transporting travelers regularly, it would have been insane to pass up an opportunity to take a few things for the less wealthy." I shrug, recalling how easy it was to smuggle items out from several of the wagons waiting to pass through the magical gateway. "Anyway, what better way to get back at her family for killing my dad and my older brother than to let her sister have a happy life without her?"

"I don't blame you at all." Jody shakes her head and rolls her eyes. "We'll need a plan of action once we make it to port. We took a lot of damage and there's a storm moving in." She plops down in the chair across from my desk as I move to the other side and sit in the captain's chair. It's a worn chair but the cushions are still comfortable.

We've always kept things informal when it's the two of us. Best friends since diapers, inseparable once walking, we've always been a package deal. Once we even stole away on my father's ship together when we were fifteen to prove we could handle ourselves on the open water. My dad was furious. It was years later that Pan and his family attacked us and brought that stupid crocodile with them. The thing finally got the rest of my father and my brother Jones. Pan's eldest skewered my brother as he tried to help my father escape the crocodile which caused them both to perish. I avenged him years later.

I cross my arms as I lean back in my chair. "Are there enough funds in the account to cover fixing the damages? Did we manage to gather enough gold on that last run? Also, do we have enough manpower to get us quickly out of harm's way?"

Jody leans forward and grabs a stack of papers to my right. She thumbs through them for a few minutes, pursing her lips as she looks.

"There's enough to cover the mast, but we may have to get creative with some of the other repairs. I'll have to check the crew before we push hard to arrive at the closest port."

"How creative are we talking? Hopefully, the crew isn't too beat up." I groan and rub a hand against my head.

"I don't know. Once we get into port we'll find out. Maybe this port will be cheaper than our usual stops?"

"Let's hope." I turn and glare out of the window. "What should we do about the Sparrow? I've grown tired of her games. I think it's time we stop that family once and for all."

Jody snorts. "How do you expect to do that, Silver? Even your father and brother couldn't do it before, and how would your new sister-in-law feel about that?"

I let out a heavy sigh and turn to face my friend. "I didn't say we had to kill any of them. The Sparrow is the only one that bothers us. She's the only one that needs to be stopped. I mean, would they really miss her if she were gone? How big is that family now? Didn't most of them leave the island once Pan passed?"

"I guess you're right, it doesn't matter what her family thinks. How do we know another of them won't come after us after we put a stop to her?"

I sigh heavily as my shoulders tense. Her words irk me but she's thinking this through better than me. I just want to be left alone to sail the waters. It's enough to have lost my family's home when my father passed. "Good point. Maybe there is something we can find that will take the magic away from her and can be used on others if needed."

Jody tilts her head to the side confused. "I thought they could fly because of pixie dust, not magic?"

"Is it really pixie dust, though? I think we should find something that will counteract their ability to fly regardless if it's magic or dust. Make them immune to whatever it is and therefore make them incapable of flying."

Jody beams. "That's a bit brutal but I like it. Then she won't be able to attack us out on the water. None of them would."

I slap my hand on the desk in excitement. "Exactly! Now let's get out there and see how the crew is doing with the ship and figure out how fast we can get to port. We need to get them rowing if we're going to make it out ahead of the storm."

I push up from my chair, eager to put our plan into action and move toward the door. Jody follows my lead and together we march back out to the deck. We've got a good amount of rowing to do, to make it to Ciara before dark, and beat the storm. I can only hope that the sea gods will bless us with a safe and speedy trip.

Chapter 2

Walking across the worn-out wood of the boat dock, I focus on my goal to find someone to aid us in our mission. The water is calm and the gentle sound of it lapping at the docks blends with the noise coming from the local market. Several small booths with fish and nets peek out of an alley that opens next to a ramshackle shop. A small wooden sign featuring an engraving of a ship hangs above its door.

Leaving my crew on the ship, with my second mate Orlando, I scan the small pier around me as I move beyond the shop. The structures are worn down and have minor damage from the storm. They look somewhat promising for the things we need and I should be able to restock the ship. We were lucky to make it to the bay and throw out the anchor as the clouds finally unleashed their rage. I sent a prayer up to the sea gods from within my cabin for letting us make it before it got worse.

Jody sprung off in search of a repairman immediately upon arriving at the dock and to aid in gathering supplies. With her help, I'm free to do what I need. There must be someone here who can help me find a way to counteract the use of pixie dust. I don't necessarily want to kill them all, I just want them to leave me and my family in peace. It's been years since we had that; and maybe get them off my family's island. Everyone deserves peace and it's high time my family had some.

I purse my lips thinking of how the Pans have been a thorn in my family's side as I walk into the dusty market full of stalls. Individuals of all kinds sell their wares but nothing catches my eye. There's got to be someone on this small island who works with magic.

I continue moving down the path, ignoring people as they vie for my attention. If I don't make eye contact with them, they won't suck me in, I remind myself as one particularly loud gentleman talks at me about cloaks as I pass. That's their secret to gaining customers, eye contact. I smile as I spot a booth at the end of the rows where two women rest against the wall. They aren't yelling at passersby to stop at their stall but gaze out with knowing looks at the small crowd.

Little bottles dangle from strings tied to the wooden cross beams holding the tarp over their booth and rest on the table before them. Incense smoke dances in the air and the sweet scent pulls at me. It's hard to identify what it is but my heart races as the possibility of them being able to help me surges through my mind. I think I've finally found someone who can work with magic. After all, their small booth appears to have all kinds of spell jars, and those jars may contain something I need.

I step up to the booth with a carefree smile on my face. My long brown hair blows behind me and the younger woman stands up. Her beauty stuns me, and I blink to regain my focus as my palms begin to sweat. I fight the urge to gape at her and remember my task. I need to get what I need and get out before I do something reckless.

"Hello, what can we do for you?" She lifts her hand and pushes her long black hair behind her shoulder. It makes me notice how vibrant and green her eyes are. I also can't help but glance down at her soft curves. It's been ages since anyone has caught my attention the way she has.

Her clothes cling to her figure and leave little to the imagination. Her skin reminds me of the ocean when calm, dark and smooth. What would it feel like beneath my hand?

"Hi," I say, clearing my throat and forcing myself to focus. "I was looking for someone who could help me with a magical problem."

She lifts her brow. "What kind of issue do you have? My grandmother and I are the only ones on the island who deal with magic."

I smile, thankful I've found them. "Well, I've an issue with someone that uses pixie dust and I need something to help counter-act it. Neutralize it, so to speak, permanently."

"Really? I haven't dealt with pixie dust but I'm sure we can figure something out, Grandmother?" I watch as the woman turns and speaks over her shoulder. "Do you know of anything that works against pixie dust?"

I watch as the older woman stands from the ground. Her joints pop audibly as she reaches her full height, and her silver hair cascades down her back. She limps toward us with a contemplative look on her face gripping her wooden cane as if her life depended on it.

"Why do you need to counteract pixie dust? They're usually harmless." She comes to a stop and flicks her hair out of her eyes as she looks me up and down.

I frown, how much should I share? "Well, it's not an issue with the pixies, but with someone who uses their dust to make themselves fly."

"Hmph. I see." The old woman frowns before turning to the younger one. "I think we may have something, Cicely, but you may be the only one that can activate it."

Cicely looks surprised. "Why does it require me to activate it?"

"It needs someone who knows how to perform magic and has the power in their blood. This woman doesn't appear to have either of those."

I shake my head. "I don't. She's right. Can you make it and I'll take it with me?"

"She has to be present with the items used for this, young

captain," the crone grits out as if a pain has taken residence in her back. "This type of magic must be activated as close as possible to its time of use otherwise it will fail."

I frown. "Are you comfortable being on a ship?"

Cicely looks at me suspiciously. "Why do you need to stop this person? Did you do something to them? Are they seeking revenge? I need to know more before agreeing to help if I must go and cast this spell."

"Does it matter, dear? Go help this woman. You'll pay well, of course?" The old woman turns to me.

"Yes. Of course, nothing is free." I lean against the stall, waiting for the women to decide.

"Very well. Cicely, we've been looking to get you off this island anyway. You know I don't have much time left, it's only fair that you go with them. You can find life on another island, and love." The old woman turns her head looking off behind with glazed over eyes.

"Bu, Grandmother, I don't want to. I don't want to leave you on your own. You need someone to help take care of you and I don't know if this woman has evil intent." Cecily places her hands on her hips and scowls at her grandmother.

"Oh posh, I'll be fine and if I die, I die. This is your chance to get off this small island and practice what I've taught you. I can see the spirits around this woman, and she doesn't have ill intent. She has the task of returning balance to something and restoring something that was once great. I can see it in her spirits as they move."

Cecily lets out a heavy sigh. "Fine. I'll do it."

I blink, taking in the rare moment between the two, realizing there's more going on than what I thought, but I still get someone for the job. The pixie dust flying fiend will be out of my hair and this woman will be paid well, and get off the island. Couldn't be that bad, right? "So, I guess our transaction needs to end. Do I pay you now or when the job is done? How does this work?"

"Oh no dearie," the grandmother says, "you'll take my granddaughter here and once the job is done, of course, you'll pay her. All you need to give me is a small fee of 15 gold pieces."

"Very good. Since I'll be taking on another mouth to feed on the ship, paying you following the job works best. Well then, I guess I'd better take you to the ship and show you where you'll be staying. Know that you'll have to help while aboard the ship. The tasks won't be difficult, of course, but no one gets free rides on the ship, even if we're paying you to do a job."

"What kind of ship do you run exactly?" Cicely squints her eyes and purses her lips.

I grin. "I work in the trade business. It'll be a great experience for you."

Cicely smirks and then looks at her grandmother. "I'll find a way to check on you."

Her grandmother nods. "I know, dear, I've seen it in the cards. Now, Captain, I do believe someone will meet you at your ship soon. You better get repairs moving. Cecily will be there shortly."

I arch a brow as her words catch me off guard. What has this woman seen? Is someone really meeting me at the ship? "Right, I'll be off."

"Alright, dear." The older woman smiles, revealing several missing teeth.

I reach into my cloak and pull out a small bag filled with coins. I pass it over to the woman who snatches it greedily before weighing it in her hand. She nods once before opening the bag and grabbing a gold piece. Biting into it she chuckles merrily before placing it back in the bag and sliding it into a pocket.

"It's settled, captain. Now off with you!" She shoos me with both her hands like a child.

I roll my eyes having been dismissed by the old hag and start making my way to the ship. Who could possibly meet me? Jody oversees repairs. Could it be someone she sent over?

I scan those around me watching for thieves. You never know what lurks in these towns and since I've exchanged coins, it's possible that someone could be watching me. One can never be too cautious.

Dust swirls around me as a light breeze carries the scent of the sea. Soon my ship comes into view and, as the hag mentioned, a gentleman with a bag stands, watching my approach. He smiles as my eyes meet his.

"Hello, Captain Silver James, I'm Norman. Jody sent me to speak with you about ship repairs. I can have repairs completed quickly but my payment must be that you supply me safe passage to your next destination." He sticks out a hand and I grab it, offering a firm shake.

I look him over, trying to figure out his character. He's dressed shabbily with holes in his long linen shirt. His hair is long and tied back from his face, which appears clean at least. His beard is long and tied with string to create a braid. Something about him bothers me, and I can't put my finger on it.

I shake my head lightly and chuckle softly. "That sounds ideal. How about we board the ship? You can get straight to work."

"Yes ma'am!"

I lead Norman to the ship in silence. I can't help but cringe at the damage as we board. The Swift Lady has seen better days. We were lucky to have made it into port, let alone make it through the storm without losing the mast completely. It should be resting at the bottom of the bay, but the gods were watching over us.

"Wow, you really took a beating, huh?"

I growl. "Don't remind me. I'll give you a quick tour and show you where you'll bunk. Anything you see or hear stays on the ship, or it'll be your death. There are secrets we keep that no ear should ever hear."

He gulps loudly and nods in understanding.

Feeling reassured, despite the weird vibe he gives me, I smile and usher him forward. "Follow me."

Chapter 3

The following day I find myself pacing the main deck of the ship, cursing under my breath. Cecily has yet to show, and I'm worried I wasted my time and money. Did that old crow take it and the two ran? She was supposed to be here last night.

The weather is pleasant with a good breeze that should carry us away from port easily, but I need the witch before we leave. My plan to take down the Sparrow is null without her.

A sharp bird's cry fills the air and I look up at Bartee, my crow's nest man, and see him pointing toward the pier. I move to the rail and pause stunned at the beauty walking toward my ship.

My heart moves to my throat and I gape as all my saliva glands seem to dry up. I stare unabashedly as her hips sway side to side with each step. She wears a tight pair of trousers, a loose grey linen shirt, a long overcoat, and a wide-brimmed hat. Her hair is pulled back into a braid that hangs on her shoulder past her breast, and she has a large pack on her back.

I cup my hands around my mouth as I reign myself in and yell out, "It's about time you showed up. You were due here yesterday."

She squints at me and shrugs. "I'm here now. May I come aboard, Captain?"

"You may." I nod and move toward the plank lowered to the dock to create a ramp. I plan to assist her safely aboard if needed. Her curves stir a fire within me, and I can't help but want to touch her. I'm not used to this sensation, and I have a feeling it's going to be a challenge to keep my hands to myself while she's on my ship.

I press my lips together to hide my thoughts and offer my hand to her. She steps over the rail, ignoring it. Instead, she smiles at me and moves stubbornly past me to the deck of the ship. Defiant and independent. Holy hell am I in trouble with this one.

"So, where will I be staying? You surely won't have me bunking with the rest of your sailors."

I glance around at the few members on deck as they cast curious glances my way. They know I sought help from someone, but little information was shared. Would they try something on her? I know we have a few female sailors, but they're tough. Cecily is different, she seems softer, not sea-worn like the rest of us.

I meet her gaze. "There is an extra bed in my quarters you can have. I'll show you to it."

I turn on my heel and quickly lead her to the door that goes to my cabin. I want her to feel comfortable aboard my ship. She may be the only person that can stop the Pan family.

"Wow, this isn't very large. How do you sleep in here?"

I laugh. "You'll get used to it. I also do my work here. If you're not comfortable with it, I can speak to Jody. She has a small bunk area set up for the few women on the crew. I think the only space available is the floor though."

I watch as she looks at the two small beds pushed next to each other across the room. They rest against a bookshelf and beneath the only window in my cabin.

"I guess this'll work. You don't snore, do you?"

"No idea." I shrug. "You can set your items under the bed. We should be ready to sail out by tomorrow morning, I hope."

"Thanks, I do have a couple of things being dropped off shortly. Grandmother is sending extra ingredients for the spell vials. She wants us to succeed. Apparently, she had a run-in with someone from Neverland with pixie dust in the past and things didn't end well."

"That's not surprising. If you don't mind, I've got some things to work on. Feel free to make yourself comfortable." I move away from her to the desk and sit trying to pull myself from staring at her. I need to go over inventory again and make sure we have plenty to cover all the mouths aboard the ship so hopefully that will give me time to collect myself.

I hear her setting things down and moving the bed. It creaks as she scoots it across the floor. She didn't have that many items on her, so is she moving the beds apart?

"Aren't you going to show me around the ship?"

Her words startle me, and I pause my internal rambling. "Right. Yes. We'll do that before I get bogged down for the next few hours. We'll start on the upper deck."

She stays at my side during the tour asking an occasional question. She seems to be taking everything in and I can't help but be mesmerized by the small bit of hair she keeps twirling around her finger. Is she nervous? Focused? What does that small quirk mean?

I continue to watch her slight movements as we finish the tour at the patched-up mast. Norman rests at its base sweating. "Hello, ladies, a fine day we're having."

I lift my brow and look at him hard. "Norman, if you want to remain on my ship, you'll address me correctly."

He sputters and nods his head. "My apologies, Captain."

Cecily laughs. "You're the first one to bring out her captain's side for me. Thank you for overstepping your boundaries, sir. It was fun to watch. I take it you're new aboard this ship as well?"

I cross my arms and look between Cecily and Norman. Did she find that cute? I didn't. It was quite frustrating and disrespectful.

"I am, Miss; sorry, I didn't catch your name." Norman continues to keep his gaze downward.

"Oh, no worries. I'm Cecily. Here to help."

"Norman's here to help as well, although he is a day behind

what he told me he could do." I continue to scowl at him.

Norman gulps. "I am and I apologize. The ship was worse off than I originally thought. This has caused a need for more repairs. We'll be sailing at dawn though. I'll get straight back to work."

"Good. Cecily, how about we return to my quarters? I'll get you a meal, then you can freshen up before checking the items left for you."

Cecily offers a small nod to Norman before turning to me. "Did they put the items in your cabin?"

I gently grab her forearm, noticing how smooth her skin feels, and lead her away from Norman. "They did."

"Excellent. I'll start sorting through them straight away."

"If you insist. I'll leave you to it while I work on some paperwork. I think I've put it off long enough."

We walk together into my cabin, and I head straight to the desk noticing another document atop my stack with food purchases. Jody must have made another round to get supplies. Excellent. Now to make sure we have enough, but what is this I see. An unusual number stands out at the bottom of the list next to rum. We usually keep some aboard, but this number doesn't seem right.

Distracted with that thought, I dig around through the papers on my desk in search of the previous list of acquired materials. There has to be something to tell me why we need so much more rum.

We sit quietly for a time as I shuffle through papers, before there's a knock at my door. Before I can respond, Jody pushes through carrying a tray of food. "Hi, thought I would intrude and meet our newest shipmate. I'm Jody."

I beam at Jody and her pushy self as Cecily responds. I lost myself in searching for that list and forgot about getting dinner for us. Where is my brain today?

"I'm Cecily, nice to meet you." She sets the book she was holding down and moves across the cabin to intercept Jody with the food. "Here let me help you with that."

"Thanks, I'm excited to see what you have in store for our little problem." Jody smiles at Cecily as she hands her some food.

Then she swings her gaze to me. "Silver, did you get a chance to go through the items I added today?"

I roll my eyes. "I did and, Cecily, just so you know, Jody is my first mate and the only one who talks with me like this. You may also speak with me informally, but I do not want this from my crew. This happens behind this door only or if we are alone."

Jody's eyebrows arch curiously at my words as Cecily responds. "I put that together. So, your first name is Silver. That's a unique name. Pretty also."

"Thank you. My mother picked it out, or so I was told. Jody, the extra supplies on the list, were they for ship repairs? I don't recall needing an increased amount of booze for repairs."

Jody sighs and sets the remaining food down on my desk. She then plops into her usual chair. "That's what I came to talk about. The only way I could bribe the gentleman we have fixing things was to provide booze and a free ride off the island. I found him hungover outside a tavern where he was dumped."

I rub my head, knowing that may have been part of the vibe I got off Norman. "Why did you think that would be a good idea?"

She shrugs. "You said we needed to get creative and the men in the bar pointed him out. They told me he's the only man left on the island to repair ships and that the other man who does repairs wouldn't be back for two weeks. He asked for strange payment, but it was cheaper to buy booze and offer him a free ride than to wait two weeks."

I flop my head back against the top of my chair and groan at the ceiling. "Well, at least it got fixed and he seems to be fixing other things I didn't realize were broken. If he can control himself, he should be fine."

Jody nods. "That was part of the agreement between he and I. He had to limit the amount he drank each day to keep from being sloppy or I threatened to toss him into the ocean."

"Who are you guys talking about?" Cecily asks curiously while twirling her hair.

I glance over to see she's gently eating her food as if it's the most precious thing in the world. It makes me wonder if she and her grandmother had trouble finding food. "The gentleman we met earlier. He spoke out of place."

Her eyes spark in understanding. "Oh, him. Got it. Sorry, I won't intrude anymore."

Jody waves a hand at her. "You're fine dear. It's nice to have another join in on the conversation at times. Silver and I've been friends for years, so it's quite refreshing. Did you know our parents worked together on a different ship?"

I roll my eyes, knowing Jody is about to give Cecily a ride down memory lane. I hope she's ready to be here for a while if she starts sharing this story.

"Really? Tell me more. I love to hear stories."

Jody leans forward in her chair eagerly as she grabs her cup. "Get comfortable because this is going to be a long one." She takes a sip from her cup and smiles. "Silver and I are daughters to the greatest pair of pirates to ever pirate these waters. They used to control all the waters of Neverland."

I laugh. "Jody, don't exaggerate. They weren't that great."

She scoffs at my words. "They were too! Silver's father was the best one-handed pirate around and my father was just as good being the first mate. They squandered jewels, gold, and so much more from ships all throughout these waters. They were the most feared pirates for a long time until they met William Pan. He caused quite a complication for them."

I sit forward and place my elbows on the desk noting how into the story Cecily seems to be. "They were feared, yes, but Pan became an issue when he found himself stuck on the island where my father kept his treasure hidden. My family and Jody's once lived on the island of Neverland before the Pans took it over. William didn't like what my father was doing even though my father was the one who rescued his ungrateful butt from the water. For some reason, on that island, William lost his memories. Then all these young boys started appearing out of nowhere. It was strange."

Jody chuckles. "I thought some of them were cute when we were younger but then William organized them to chase our families from the island. They kicked everyone out of the town our fathers built. Despite it being a town full of pirates it was a safe

21

place to grow up. We all looked after each other. We had a code to do so."

"Why did he chase you guys out? He never got his memories back?" Cecily scrunches her eyebrows together in the cutest way after asking her question.

I shrug as Jody frowns, then I take a deep breath before letting it out slowly. This information is something my father never shared with anyone but me. "The secret to why he kicked us out was that he fell for a girl one of the pirates found at sea. She had her two younger brothers with her, and the man was a complete gentleman to them. He brought them in and helped them recover from being dehydrated. The girl met William while out for a walk one day and he became smitten. He was determined to get her away from us."

I groan and lean back as Jody watches me. "Around that time, my father had a higher-ranking pirate executed. He didn't tell anyone the full story, only that he broke a forbidden rule. I only happened to learn about this after walking in on him talking to my older brother about it. My brother Jones had saved the young woman from being used further by the pirate. He tried to rape her. She took her brothers and ran after the execution and that's when Pan's group began to push us out. It took years for him to accomplish it but we were forced away regardless."

"Oh my, I didn't realize that's what happened! Why did you never tell me this?" Jody voices with her hands on her cheeks and brows lifted.

I shake my head and let out a sigh. "It's not a pleasant thing to recall honestly, and I was forbidden to share it back then. After we were run out of our small pirate town, Pan spelled the crocodile that took my father's arm to finish the rest of him. My father died trying to get us away from the island safely. My oldest brother died with him. A few of Pan's family continue to harass us now because another brother of mine ran off with one of William's daughters."

Cecily sits staring at me with her mouth agape. "That is so stupid. Now I know why my grandmother disliked people from Neverland. Her father used to pirate as well. I wonder if he was one of the few living there before?"

"Who knows? He could have been." I reach out for some of the food.

"Anyway, that's basically the gist of the story. I'll spare you more tales for tonight, Cecily. My mind is blown by the tidbit of what caused Pan to go bananas." Jody crosses her arms and glares at me. "Even though I'm upset you kept that from me all these years, I'm glad you finally shared it."

I look down at the desk as I nibble on my food. Memories flood through my head of walking in on my brother distraught and pacing before my father as he shared the story. I look back up at Jody. "That is part of why I pushed us into rescuing women who are abused on top of our pirating. I know we haven't saved many but it's the least we can do, right?"

She nods. "Right. Well, I'll leave you two for the night. I'm going to get some rest before my watch in the morning. Have a good night, ladies."

"Thanks for the food, Jody." Cecily holds up her cup in farewell.

"Get some rest, old friend." I wave as Jody disappears through the door.

"I can't believe all that happened to your family. If you don't mind me asking though, why do you steal from others?"

I smile at her words. "Pirating is all I've ever known and, really, we don't take from certain ships. We scout out those that are run by vile individuals and hit them. That's a secret though, so never tell anyone. My ship has a solid, if somewhat fibbed, reputation on these seas."

She laughs heartily. "Well, your secret is safe with me. Are you going to bed soon?"

I rub my eyes and pause realizing exactly how tired I am. "I probably should. Telling that old story wore me out."

"Oh, that's good to hear. I have a hard time sleeping when a candle is lit. Something about the light makes it difficult to fall asleep."

"So, you're a light sleeper?"

She chuckles. "Only if a candle is lit, otherwise I sleep like the dead."

I stand from my chair and stretch. "Alright, let's call it a night. We'll both need our energy tomorrow."

Chapter 4

The following day I stand on the quarter deck of my ship as the sales billow out in the strong breeze. I had us moving out across the water a little after dawn following Jody's check on the main mast. Norman did a fine job fixing it and celebrated late into the night. He was still passed out beneath the stairs next to his box of tools. It worries me but he was able to complete his job so I guess I can cut him some slack.

I smile thinking about how Jody and I bonded with Cecily last night during our shared meal. Cecily seems so sweet but has a tough exterior when surrounded by a group of people. I'm glad she felt comfortable around us, and it surprised me I felt comfortable with her. Is it because I'm attracted to her?

I glance down as I spot Cecily running for the rail of the ship. She grips the edge before leaning over. My heart stutters as I fear she's leaned too far when the sound of her retching hits me. Oh no, she's seasick! I frown as she continues to hang on to the side. What was it my father used to give me when I struggled to adjust to the waters as a young girl? It was some type of herb. Oh, right he had me drink peppermint and ginger tea.

Puckering my lips, I run through the list of items we picked up at port, in my head, trying to recall if we picked up any of those ingredients. I know the cook uses a lot of things to make meals with, so we should have them.

I turn to look over my shoulder and snag Orlando's gaze. He's an excellent second mate and one of the only few people I trust to steer my ship. "Hey, O, take over for me, I need to stretch my legs."

He perks up and scuttles over. "Yes, ma'am, Captain James."

I nod before walking over to the steps that lead me down to the deck and walk quickly to the ladder that drops into the hold. Grunting as I reach the bottom, I make my way to the makeshift kitchen to find the herbs, before grabbing a cup of the water boiling on a small flame. Cook and I worked out a deal where she could make us hot meals but the fire had to be contained. The magic cauldron she snagged from a traveler made it manageable. It keeps the flames from harming the ship and lets her cook safely.

Holding the steaming cup close to me, I drop the herbs in and swirl them around. They float gently in a circle as I move the cup, making a small whirlpool. Smiling and feeling content that I have something that will help, I head back to the main deck, where I find Cecily seated next to the rail with Norman at her side.

I glare at the vile man and grit my teeth. The hand holding the cup of tea tightens as I fight the urge to punch him. I push the emotions down and plaster a smile on my face. I have no claim to this woman and there's no reason to stir up trouble. "Everything all right here?"

Norman's gaze shoots up at my words and I notice how bloodshot his eyes are. "I heard this angel losing her stomach over the side. Just thought I'd sit with her."

Cecily looks up at me, still a little pale, and offers me a slight smile. "I didn't know that being on the water would bother me like this."

I nod in understanding and offer her the cup. "Here, drink

some of this, it should help."

She reaches out and gently takes it, holding it to her nose. I try not to laugh when she sniffs it. "What is it?"

"It's only tea. Ginger mixed with peppermint to be exact. Something that will help with your nausea."

Norman coughs to get our attention. "My mother used to give that type of mix to me as a boy when we would go on my father's boat to fish. It'll help and it tastes good."

Cecily nods and then places the cup to her lips. She sips and her shoulders drop. A bit of color returns to her face and she smiles faintly. "It does taste good. Thank you, Captain."

"You're very welcome. Norman, now that you're up, I do believe Jody has some tasks for you."

He pushes up from sitting next to Cecily. "Yes, Captain. I'll report to her right away." I frown as he gives Cecily a lingering look before walking off.

"Can you help me back to the cabin area, Captain? I think I need to lie down for a bit."

"I can, Cecily. You should adjust to the water in a few days' time. I'll make sure the cook keeps tea made for you."

She nods. "Thank you, I do appreciate it. I'll look and see if there is something in one of the spell books that will help as well. This is horrible. I'm also disappointed that I didn't think to look for a spell before boarding the ship. My grandmother warned me something like this could happen."

I chuckle knowing full well how it feels to be seasick. "It can be miserable, but I'll take care of you. I can tell now that you haven't been out on the sea much."

She shakes her head. "No, Grandmother and I never had a way to travel on the water and we couldn't afford it. It was enough to have food on the table regularly. Most of the time we ate what we foraged in the area. Occasionally she would bargain her way onto a small fisherman's boat but nothing more."

I nod, listening. "Well, you're more than welcome to anything on the ship. In a bit, when your stomach is settled, you should eat some bread. Nothing too heavy for the next few days though."

"That's a good idea." We reach the door, and she pushes it open before I can get it for her. "Silver, I must ask, are you normally this kind to all your guests? You don't seem to like that Norman character."

I close the door and turn to face her as she watches me intently. "No, I'm not usually kind to any guest." I shrug. "I don't trust others easily. There's something about you, though, that makes me feel calm. I like it and I feel that I can trust you. You seem like a genuinely good person."

"I like to think I am but why me?"

I tilt my head contemplating her words momentarily. "I don't have an answer to that other than I'm attracted to you. I hope that doesn't freak you out."

She smiles. "Why would it freak me out? I'm attracted to you too."

I pause as her word register. She's attracted to me? What? "I'm not sure how to respond to that."

"I guess there isn't anything to say. We barely know each other, so would you be interested in building on that attraction?"

I blink trying to sort out an answer. My mind is spinning, and my body feels light. I would, yes, but she's going to leave after we deal with the Pans, isn't she? "I guess we can see where it goes."

She grabs my hand. "I'd like that. Now if you don't mind, I'm going to lie down."

I laugh as she lets go of my hand and moves to the bed. "Okay. I'll come to check on you in a bit and see if you're ready for some bread. I'll send Cook up with more tea for you to sip on in the meantime."

She waves her hand before plopping down on the bed and pulling the small pillow over her eyes to block out the light. She looks cute as she gets comfortable, and I let myself out of the door. Once I get the tea figured out, I take my time checking the crew before returning to the quarter deck.

Chapter 5

After a full day of work and navigating the ship, I turn over my job to Naga, my night lady as I like to call her, to keep an eye on things. Despite her meek appearance with brown hair and eyes, she has a wicked tongue and keen sight. She can spot danger a mile away but has always worked best at night. It's always made me wonder if she's more than human. She's never shared much about her past but then again if you're not a danger to me or my crew I never check into one's past too much. We've all made mistakes in life. She's always had a pleasant vibe around her which I learned to trust long ago.

I take a few deep breaths of the salty air as I make my way down the steps toward my door. The tension in my shoulders eases and my muscles feel heavy. The cool night air is refreshing, causing more tension to leave my body, and I can only hope that Cecily is feeling better than she did earlier. The small window in my cabin usually lets in a good breeze, which should help with nausea.

Pushing through my wooden door, I'm stopped in my

tracks as I see Cecily. She has the beds pushed close to the window and is leaning back with her head resting on the wall, chin turned slightly toward the window. Her hair falls loosely around her shoulders, and she wears nothing but her undergarments.

My cheeks heat and my heart pounds as I stare. She's sleeping in an odd position, and I watch her chest slowly rise and fall. It's calming, making my heart rate slow a bit, and I force myself forward, closing the door gently. I don't want to wake her, so I tip toe to my desk area to prepare for the night.

Sitting on my chair at the desk to pull off my boots, I freeze as it creaks, seeming to echo in the small cabin. My heart picks up speed again while I hold my breath. Did that wake her?

With a silent prayer, I glance over to see she's still sleeping and continue to undress. Feeling cooler after removing layers, I move toward the beds. I crawl across the mattress toward her resting form and gently wrap my arms around her to move her to a more comfortable position.

As I lift gently her eyes pop open, and she sits up causing me to drop my hold. "Silver?"

"Hey, Cecily, I didn't want to wake you, but I also didn't want you to get cramps sleeping like that. How are you feeling?"

She stretches and yawns before moving to a different position on the bed. Laying back on the mattress and rolling to her side, she lets out a soft sigh. "I feel better, just tired. I didn't mean to fall asleep by the window, but I also didn't want to dirty up your things if I got sick. The window made it easier to do that."

I frown. "I see. So, the tea didn't help?"

She moves again and pats the mattress motioning me to lie down. "It did, but my stomach was still unsettled. I managed to find a spell that should help, though, between bouts of nausea. I'll get the ingredients for it tomorrow from Cook and from my bags. I didn't have the energy to attempt it."

"You found a spell? That's excellent, not that we have a lot of people on board who get seasick, but this will be beneficial for you!"

She nods. "It'll make a huge difference. How was your day?"

I move and lay on my side next to her, smiling as our eyes meet. "It was uneventful. Everyone stayed on task and there weren't any threats. Makes for an easygoing day."

"Do you frequently get attacked on the water?"

I mull her question over. There have been more attacks by the Sparrow recently but no other pirates. "No, but lately there has been a slight increase. We normally seek out other pirates on the water, which I wouldn't consider as threats. We're the ones they should fear."

She frowns. "Do these attacks correlate to this job you have me working on?"

I nod. "They do. Hopefully, we won't have any until we arrive to finish the pixie dust issue. It will give us an edge if she doesn't know we're coming."

"Yes, it would. I don't want her or anyone in her group discovering our plans."

"I agree. Speaking of plans, do you have an idea of what to use yet?"

She shakes her head and plops it back on the soft surface of the bed. "Not yet, but once I'm feeling better, I can start working on some things. Mixing something to counteract the pixie dust isn't exactly a common spell. It'll be more difficult to put together than I thought. My grandmother didn't exactly help with any ideas before we left either. She was way too eager for me to join this adventure."

"Do you think you'll need other ingredients than what we have?" I tilt my head contemplating the places we could stop on our way to Neverland. Maybe we could sail to Mortiki, they normally have things from other countries at their port.

"I don't think so, but I'll know more once I start mixing. I should have a bit of everything already. Most of the boxes I brought with me are filled with dried herbs, liquids, and other items to aid me."

"Well, if you discover we need something let me know." I snuggle down on the mattress pulling the thin blanket to my shoulders.

"Silver," Cecily says hesitantly, reaching out a hand and

placing it on my arm. "Will you hold me?"

I blink at her trying to process her words. "Are you sure?"

"Yes." She lets a soft breath escape from her lips. "I'm sure."

I slide closer to her letting the hand she has resting on me fall across my back. She scoots in and rests her head on my arm as I wrap it beneath her. I smile as she lets out a deep sigh of contentment. It makes my insides dance knowing that I can bring this small bit of comfort to her. I rest my head on top of hers and as she falls asleep, I close my eyes.

The sensation of having a body next to me is strange but it feels right. It's different from when I shared a bed with my siblings as a kid. Our home wasn't large so many of us shared giant pallets. This though, with Cecily, the fact she already trusts me to keep close is astounding. If I let her have my heart, will I end up hurt in the end?

Shaking my head gently, to keep from disturbing sleeping beauty, I force an end to my thoughts. I can only focus on now and what is occurring. Thinking of what-ifs can lead to a dangerous game.

Please goddess Nominkki, let her be gentle with my heart. I've had enough pain to span multiple lifetimes. I remain calm and focus inward as I send my prayer out to the goddess. Hopefully, she'll hold me close as I navigate these waters with Cecily.

Chapter 6

Sweat slides down the back of my neck as I stare out across the open water days later, lost in my thoughts. It's been a relatively calm morning, but the sun has become brutal. The meager breeze helps but do I dare pray for rain?

Cecily sits nearby with a large book and several vials of liquid. Who knows what she's mixing? She's continued to struggle with finding something to use against our foe. It's made us all anxious. Will she have something to use by the time we reach Neverland?

Cecily has been managing her sea sickness with the tea Cook and I keep ready for her, and the potion she mixed with simple ingredients, that we thankfully had on board. It also needed a bit of sea water, which we have more than enough of. Such a strange ingredient. After the first day on it, her color came back, and she was able to move around more.

She and I have spent more time chatting about our lives as well. She told me her parents died when she was young, and her grandmother raised her. She had a hard life back on the island, but since I found her and asked for her help, she has hope for the first time. Hope that life isn't always scrounging around for food and trying to sell enough spells to pay for things.

I keep my eyes focused on the sea as I steer but every once and a while I glance up and catch Norman staring Cecily down. The lad appears infatuated with her but the look in his eyes suggests questionable intentions. It worries me and I refuse to let Cecily out of my sight. He's also been hitting the booze hard, disregarding his agreement with Jody, the last few days. She and I have had words about it, but she hopes he'll stop soon. There are still things that need fixing, and he's done a great job on that at least. I don't understand why she's giving him the benefit of the doubt.

I frown as his eyes seem to shift. I know that look he has now, and it scares me. I should have quizzed Jody about him before we left port and forced her to find someone else even if it would have meant waiting. His look is predatory and, currently, he's not sober.

I remain where I am, jaw clenched, as Norman moves across the deck with a determined look on his face. He calls out a greeting to Cecily and she glances up, offering him a wary smile. Does she pick up on the slime beneath his attractive exterior or is it just me? Does she know his true intent or am I overthinking it?

Norman sits next to Cecily, and she scoots distinctly away from him. He frowns and moves closer before trying to engage her in conversation. Cecily nods but I smile as she stands, moving quickly away, saying something over her shoulder as she does. It decreases my concern, but I won't feel comfortable until he's left her alone.

I watch her move further into the shadows and I know she's headed toward my cabin. At least she can have some space to work on her potions in private. I hate that she can't enjoy the fresh air while doing it. I turn to look over the deck again, but Norman standing, cursing, and following Cecily, causes me to freeze. I stiffen and my pulse picks up as my palms grow sweaty. He wouldn't, would he?

He keeps moving and I force myself forward. Like hell he's

34

entering my room with her in there. I make it to the bottom of the steps and he's nowhere to be found. My heart begins to pound now and sweat beads across my brow as I prepare myself, pushing the bit of nausea I feel down. I draw my sword and move stealthily to my door. My body trembles as fear and rage war inside of me. I place my ear against the wood and listen.

The sound of a scuffle and loud thuds reaches my ear and I force the door open. It doesn't budge. Something is behind it preventing me from opening it. No!

I yell and ram my shoulder into it once again. Some of my crew hear me and come to my aid. With the three of us the door crashes in and I find Norman with his hands on Cecily, pinning her to the floor. Her clothes are in disarray and her face is bloody.

"Get off her!" I scream running forward and placing my sword at his back. He freezes, realizing he's no longer alone and my blade is too close.

Slowly, with shoulders tense, he turns and sees me and my crewmen. His eyes widen and he moves to the side away from my blade.

He clears his throat as he stands, holding his hands in the air. "It's not what it looks like. She propositioned me. She wanted this."

"You pig. Get away from us! Take him out of here! I know exactly what to do with him." I glare at him as Cecily pushes from the floor, trying to wrap her torn clothes around her exposed body.

She stares down and scrambles back toward the wall, wrapping her arms around herself after she's managed to cover her body. Tears stream down her cheeks as she trembles. A fire ignites in my soul to see her in such a state and wrath like no other explodes.

My eyes feel like they glow as I growl out orders. "Tie him up and ready the plank. I'll be there shortly. Go."

One of my men grabs Norman roughly before taking him through the destroyed door. They are all silent as they lead him out and I try to let some of my anger out by kicking at the remaining pieces of the door. I'll have to fix that later.

I move toward Cecily and sit next to her on the ground.

"Are you okay?"

She shakes her head and leans into me. I wrap my arms around her to offer comfort. I'm not sure what else to do. Her tears turn to sobs, and I tighten my hold.

"You're safe now. I won't let him hurt you again."

She lifts her head. "Thank you. I didn't know what to do. I thought coming here would get me away from him."

I reach up and push hair out of her face. "I understand. I was worried he would try something. He had a strange look in his eye when he was watching you earlier. Are you well enough for me to deal with him?"

"What will you do?"

I smile, feeling the simmering rage within. "Oh, it's not what I'll do, but what will the seas do? He's going off the plank into the deep."

Her eyes widen and her lips for an o.

"Stay here and get cleaned up. I'll handle him and be back to check on you." I help her to stand and get her over to the chair at my desk. "Remember there are fresh towels in that drawer, and you can use some of the basin water. I'll be back."

She nods and moves toward the drawer as I step away. I hear her rustling around, grabbing the necessary items as I slip out the door.

On deck, Jody and several other crew members stand around Norman. His feet and hands are bound and will remain as such. Scum like him doesn't deserve to live.

"Well, Norman, what do you have to say for yourself?" Crossing my arms on my chest I stop before him. It takes everything I have not to punch him.

"I already told you; she wanted me to follow her. It was a game." He shrugs as best as possible with his arms bound behind his back. His bloodshot eyes stare at me and I can tell he feels no remorse for his actions.

"That was not a game. You had that glint in your eye when you walked to her, and I know that you planned it. Crew, is the plank ready?"

"Please, Captain Silver, have mercy!" Tears stream down

his face.

"Mercy? Were you showing mercy back there? I think not. Your punishment is just. You had a deal with Jody that you've neglected to keep on top of this incident. You're no longer needed here. The god of the sea will handle you now. He too does not like vile men who prey on women."

"But you're a pirate! Isn't that what you do? Don't you all take advantage of people?"

I laugh. "We are pirates, and no, that is not what we do. We steal treasures not of the flesh and aid those looking to escape such things. Filth like you is the reason we steal treasure. We take others and get them out of terrible situations. We take from those who do them wrong."

"Then you're not a pirate." He glares and spits at my feet. "Pirates steal and take what they want."

I laugh again and my crew joins in. "We know who we are. Up with you. It's time."

He yanks against my men holding him crying out as it pulls at his shoulders. They shake him aggressively and start dragging him across the deck. I smile and turn to face the large plank reaching out into the air over the sea. Water churns below it and memories of the old crocodile spin through my mind. If only he were here. I think he'd enjoy such a meal.

The water changes from waves to a small vortex that grows before our eyes. My heart stutters as I realize Tannafin, the sea god of life and justice, heard our declaration of Norman's wrongs. We've asked him in times past to deal with scum, as we've forced others into the sea, but never has he revealed his presence. It makes me wonder what else Norman has done in his life. Did he do something against the gods?

My men release Norman and swords are drawn to keep him from throwing himself back on the deck. He wobbles as he stands on the plank. Tears stream down his face and a wet stain forms across his trousers. He sobs as his body trembles. "Please. I promise not to harm another person."

I growl clenching my fists into my side. I wouldn't dare let him live now that the god has made his presence. "Go before we push you. Give yourself that dignity at least." I stand with my weight shifted to my hip. This isn't the first time I've forced someone to walk the plank, but it seems I'm the only one who's noticed the presence of Tannafin.

Norman gulps before turning and taking a small step. I hear a scream mixed with a sob break loose from him as he nears the edge and sees the vortex. His body continues to tremble, and my crew and I wait. If he tries to back up, we will push him.

With another loud sob from Norman, he steps off the end of the plank and drops into the ocean. I move to the rail and look over. Bubbles appear amidst the middle of the whirlpool and bust causing a sound akin to someone releasing a deep sigh. It causes goosebumps to spread across my skin and I close my eyes briefly before opening them to see if he'll float up from the depths. I watch for several minutes as does my crew, but he doesn't return to the surface.

"Very well, men, ladies, let's get this cleaned up. I'll be in my cabin if you need me. Oh, and someone repair my door." I turn on my heel and head back to my cabin letting my anger dissipate.

"You heard her! Everyone to work. Bort, get the door fixed for the captain immediately." Jody yells at everyone, making me smile. She's an excellent first mate and knows I'm rattled. She hasn't missed how close I've become with Cecily, and I doubt she missed the god's skills below the plank.

I quietly enter the cabin and notice Cecily sprawled on my bed. Her chest rises and falls slowly, and I can tell she's asleep. The events must have taken it out of her and I'm relieved she was able to fall asleep. I begin picking up what remains on the floor as I wind down. My brain is still running at high speed over the incident, and I remind myself she's safe.

Once things are back in order, and Bort's repaired the door as best as he could, I sit down at my desk and watch Cecily as she continues to sleep. My heart aches for what she was put through today. How dare Norman lay a hand on her like he did? I bow my head over my hands and make a promise that as long as she chooses to stay in my life, I'll keep her from going through something like that ever again.

Chapter 7

I wake to someone shaking my shoulder and notice how stiff I feel. I lift my head and blink sleepily as Cecily stares at me. She has a frown on her face and her brows are creased.

"Did you sleep there all night?"

Her words make me blink again and I look around. I'm still sitting at my desk with papers scattered everywhere. I stretch, feeling my joints pop as I do. "I guess so. I don't remember falling asleep. How are you this morning?"

She comes around behind the desk and leans in toward me. Wrapping her arms around me, I hear her let out a deep breath. "Thank you for what you did yesterday."

I wrap my arms around her in return and pull her in closer, inhaling her sweet scent. The smell of spice and herbs fills my nostrils. It must be lingering from the things she was working on. "You're welcome. I hope we never find ourselves in that situation again."

She shakes and I can imagine that she still has some fear

lingering from the attack. "Agreed. I must admit though, seeing you kick butt like you did was a turn on."

She tries to pull away from me and I hold on, using a hand to tip her chin up, so I can see her eyes. "You think so? Maybe I should do that more often." I lean in and place my lips gently on hers. They are soft despite the whipping of the wind when out on deck, which usually chaps lips. I hope mine aren't too dry.

She pulls back smiling. "I'd rather you not, honestly. What sparked that kiss?"

I slowly push from my chair into standing feeling the discomfort of my body from staying in a seated position all night. "You did. I couldn't resist. You're beautiful."

She blushes and swats my arm. "Don't say that. Neither of us have showered in days and my hair's a rat's nest."

I shake my head. "You are. Now, should we grab some food? I can have some brought to us if you would rather stay in." I use my hand to pull her back to me and move her hair over her shoulder. She holds my gaze as we stand, and heat builds between us.

"What are you thinking, Silver?" Her words are a whisper and I feel my heart race.

"I'm thinking that I want to take you to bed. I want to show you what it's like to be cared for." I lean in and kiss her.

Cecily wraps her arms around my neck and our kiss intensifies. I'm taller than her so I lift her gently as she wraps her legs around me. We move toward the beds where they're still pushed together by the window. I lay her gently back on the mattress, pulling my lips away from her, and hold myself above her.

I stare intently at her trying to calm my heart. I need to know if she's ready for this or if I'm rushing. "Are you okay with this?"

She's breathless but nods. "I'd let you know if I wasn't."

I let out my breath not realizing I'd been holding it. I then slide down to her stomach as I lift her shirt. I pepper her skin with kisses as I work her bottoms down. Her sighs of pleasure encourage me to continue, and I only pause to pull her pants completely off.

I move back up her body and slowly remove her top, so she's laid bare before me. Grabbing my arm, she pulls me down on top of her and begins to fumble with my clothes. Soon we lay next to each other sliding our hands across each other's skin. It's amazing the sensation it causes.

After minutes of exploring each other's touch, I slide back above her gently sliding my hand down to her sex. She takes a sharp breath in as I enter her folds with one finger. Using my thumb and index, stroking, and applying pressure to the right area, I bring her over the edge several times before moving in with my lips. Her scent is glorious as I explore with my tongue and her moans fuel my passion. Soon she's spiraling again, screaming my name. I lift to meet her gaze, bringing a hand to her lips to silence her, only to be flipped to my back in surprise.

I stare at her gorgeous, flushed face, and observe the predatory look in her eyes. It's not the same gaze as Norman had for her. Her gaze is filled with heated passion and a desire for more. She knows what she wants. To think I thought she was inexperienced in these matters, hah, oh, how wrong I was.

Hours later after our sweaty bodies have cooled, we dress again and flop back on the bed. I feel more relaxed than I have in ages and gods only know what the crew heard.

"I think now we need to eat." I get up from the bed and look down at her.

She ponders on my words briefly before popping up from the bed. She bends and pulls a wooden crate from beneath it. "Food sounds amazing. How far out are we from Neverland?"

I frown trying to keep up with her train of thought. "Uhm, a couple of days, why?"

She plops down on the floor and rummages around in the box. "I need to finish making the potion mix but could use an extra hand. I didn't realize we were that close. Is it okay if we stay in and bottle some of what's already made? I'll need to make more but I'm going to have to work all the next two days with some late nights to get it all ready."

I nod in understanding. "Okay, I'll go grab us some food and do what I can to help. Do you need another set of hands besides mine?"

She purses her lips. "No, your hands are perfect."

I smirk, catching her unspoken meaning. "Okay, you'll show me what to do with the mixes?"

She laughs causing my smirk to shift into a smile. "Of course, I will, silly. I wouldn't throw you into something without instructions. Any type of potion work requires steady hands and focus. Now go get us something to eat so our energy doesn't die."

I chuckle and stretch again before moving to the makeshift door. "I'll be back."

I step through the door to the deck. Everyone is in motion as if yesterday didn't happen. It makes my heart lighter knowing my crew supported me like they did on my decision. They offer smiles and waves as I make my way over to the door that leads down below deck. Cook will have something going, I'm sure.

As I step into the kitchen someone grabs my arm. I turn in surprise and realize it's Jody.

"Hey, how is Cecily this morning?" I can tell she's still concerned by her frown.

"She seems to be doing okay. She's realized she's behind on her potion making though. She thought we had more time before reaching Neverland."

"Ah, well, I'm glad she's okay. Norman was a pig. I'm sorry I made a deal with him." She frowns, dropping her shoulders. Her gaze drops to the ground, and she seems to deflate.

I place a hand on her shoulder. "It's not your fault. You were doing what you thought was best to save us some money. No one blames you."

She lets out a deep sigh. "I blame me. If I had found someone else Cecily wouldn't have been attacked. Is there anything I can do to make it up to her?"

"I really don't think that's necessary. You can ask her though. I'm just grabbing us something to eat. She and I are working on mass producing vials or something for our arrival today. I didn't think to let her know how close we were to Neverland, so she's got a lot of potion work to do."

Jody's face brightens. "Do you think she would let me join

you? This will also make it where one of us can check on the crew on occasion. Not that they need us to watch over them, but the break may be needed depending on what she has you doing."

I shrug and finish walking into the kitchen, noticing Cook is already filling bowls for me and Cecily. She must have heard me in the hall. "That's not a terrible idea."

"Great."

I nod and grab the bowls from Cook. She grumbles as I turn and head out of the kitchen and back up to the deck. Jody stays at my side until we reach my door. She opens it for me, and we enter my small cabin.

"Hey, Cecily, how are you feeling this morning? I'm sorry about yesterday. I feel terrible about what Norman did," Jody voices as I move toward the desk with food.

Cecily looks at me, then at Jody. "It's not your fault. It's not like anyone could have controlled him."

Jody frowns. "I feel bad because I'm the one who brought him in to fix things."

"Don't worry about it Jody. Silver, is it gruel again?" She moves toward me and picks up a bowl.

I nod. "Yes. There aren't many choices when out on sea. We'll find something different on land."

"We could always try to fish. Sometimes we catch something worth eating. Is there anything I can help with today, Cecily?" Jody leans on the desk as Cecily takes a chair.

"No, I think I've got everything under control with Silver helping." Cecily takes a bite of her gruel, making a strange face.

"Really though, I insist that I help somehow. It's the least I can do after what happened," Jody pleads.

Cecily sighs and I eat in silence. I'm not getting in on this conversation. "Fine, I'll have you help Silver line the bottles and fill them with the premade mixture. That'll open it up for me to make a few more batches. Maybe it will speed up the process and I can have more down time before we reach land."

Jody claps her hands. "Excellent! It's settled then."

I pause holding my spoon in the air. "What do you mean when you say line the bottles?"

Cecily smiles. "I'm going to have you draw specific runes along the bottle. It will keep it sealed until it encounters someone who has pixie dust on them."

"That's interesting. Will it work?" I ask incredulously.

"Are you doubting her work, Silver?" Jody chimes.

"Of course it'll work. I'm making extra, though, in case some of them are faulty. You can never be too prepared." Cecily finishes eating from her bowl and sets it down. "Now let me show you which bottles to use and what tools. You two are going to be busy for a while. You must line the bottles before you fill them and then draw a specific rune on the cork."

"Well then," I set my bowl down, "let's get to it."

Chapter 8

I stare out across the water as a massive mountain appears on the horizon. A small line of smoke appears near the top of the mountain, and I know instantly that we're approaching Neverland. It's covered in shades of green from light to dark, most of which hold their own magic. I remember being fascinated as a child at the interesting things the island held.

More memories of my childhood drift to the forefront of my mind. Playing in my father's ship and teasing the giant crocodile are some of my favorites. The crocodile never seemed that mean to me, but I guess I was wrong.

The smell of salt, jasmine, and incense breaks me from my memory, and I glance to my right to see Cecily leaning against the rail looking out at the land. I left her early this morning in our cabin to check on the ship. We had a busy night of making potions and taking breaks to explore our lust.

"So that's Neverland? I expected it to be more magical than that." She looks over her shoulder at me.

I snort. "What would something more magical look like?"

"A floating island with unicorns and rainbows, maybe? I

don't know, it seems so dull." Her sarcasm makes me chuckle.

I smile and lean against the rail next to her, looking out over the water. "At one point of time it had a silver fog that hung about but that's it. It's always been another normal looking island."

She tilts her head to the side causing her braid to fall. "Oh, so do you think she knows we're approaching?"

I turn my head back toward her and grin. "Maybe. Are you worried?"

She rolls her eyes. "No, I'm not worried. I'm here to help you put a stop to her pixie dust usage, right?"

I frown and reach out for her hand. She looks down at it as I entangle my fingers with hers. "I was hoping you now had a better reason to be here."

"Silver, I believe I do but are you sure this is what you want?"

I nod and pull her into me. Wrapping my arms around her, I breathe in her scent and sigh. "It's what I want. I couldn't have ever predicted this but I'm glad it happened. You'll stay with me after this is all over?"

She pushes back gently and meets my gaze. "I will but only if we can spend some time on land more often. I can't market my spells and trinkets to the crew."

I laugh. "You're right, that doesn't seem like it would work well. I'm sure we can figure it out."

"Do you have a plan for when we face off with this Sparrow?" Her sudden change in subject catches me off guard momentarily but I quickly shift my thoughts.

"If we're on the water we'll have to be quick to hit her with some of the powder you made. She may catch on that it's a trap. If we make it to dry land, we can hide several vials in the trees and use a trap to spring them loose."

Cecily nods. "Good. Now we have some type of plan. I was worried you would have me run at her screaming and try to tackle her."

"As much as I would love to see that," I laugh, "I don't want you to die by her sword." I squeeze her hand before releasing it.

"I'd rather not die as well." She turns toward me. "Is there anything I can help with to prepare for land?"

I stand straight and put my hands on my hips. I take a moment to think before I respond. "I can't think of anything other than preparing a bag to travel with your supplies. That's the most important part of this excursion."

She giggles. "When you call it an excursion, you make it sound like this will be fun."

I shrug. "It could be. We don't know what we'll come across."

Cecily twirls away from the rail smirking over her shoulder. "Well, Captain, I better get on that. Come find me shortly."

I smile and turn back to the water. I lean once again on the rail and think of what we'll do when we reach the shore. The plan for us is to dock on the southern side of the island where my father's small town used to be. As far as I know it's still vacant and a regular ghost town. We can work our way from there, having spent most of my childhood there, I know we can get water running and patch up some of the old buildings. It'll be easier for us to replenish our stores as well since we can gather fruit from the trees. Heck, if we succeed in this task, we could reinhabit the town. That would be wonderful.

I stare at the water as it splashes against the side of the ship. If we were to stop the Sparrow and build the old town back up, I could restore my family's name and tradition of running a pirate sanctuary. That's what it used to be for all of the pirates back in the day anyway. My father made sure they stuck to a specific code, and we lived well. If someone wished to do something against the town rules they were sentenced to death, at least if they didn't escape first. Could I bring the town back to its old glory and incorporate a trade route for Cecily to sell some of her items?

Chapter 9

I stay lost in my thoughts until land draws closer. The trees grow larger and light dances through their leaves of various colors. Now the old magic shows itself. Does that mean something? Is that a sign of good luck?

We make our way around the edge of the island as the strange light seems to follow us. I can't remember seeing anything like it as a kid, but it fills me with hope. Soon it disappears and old buildings catch my eye from the shore. Butterflies dance in my stomach and I bounce on my toes as the ship slows.

Minutes later, the anchor drops toward the bottom of the bay next to the old town. It's weird that it's free of all debris and only the remnants of post-marks where long docks once stood. The water is clear and fish swim beneath its depths.

Back when we all still lived here, my father had large wooden docks that reached far enough out into the bay for large ships such as mine to dock on. Small wooden structures contained extra supplies along each dock for ships to access if needed. It saved everyone some leg work, not having to haul it from town.

"Ready the boats, mates, we're rowing in!" I yell across the deck as loud as I can and get a resounding response from my crew. It's time to face the fear lingering from being pushed out of my home and I toy with what to expect as we prepare to step foot on land.

The sound of splashing snaps me from my thoughts as one of our boats is dropped into the water. We only have four, so I know that we'll have to make multiple trips. A few of the crew will remain on the ship to guard it while the others will remain with me as we enter the town. We may need more than a few people to take on the Sparrow and with her this close, it's not safe to leave the ship unattended.

"Are we ready to head to shore, Captain?" Cecily sidles up to me with a smile on her face, twirling the end of her braid.

"Yes, you'll be riding in a boat with Jody and me. We'll take the second boat to shore, after the group in the first boat has checked to make sure it's safe.

"I'm sure it'll be fine. What reason would anyone have to linger around this old place? It looks dilapidated from here."

Shrugging, I push memories of the town's former glory to the back of my mind. "It may be run down, but it was once set up to give us some of the finer things in life. You can never be too careful. Do you have everything you need?"

She turns and I see a large bag hanging from her shoulders. "Yes. This bag is full of potions. Once we're on land, I'll make sure to distribute them to those who will join our search party. The more of us that have the mix, the more likely we'll be able to hit all our targets."

I nod in approval. "Good! I hadn't considered that. Will we need to chant anything in particular when we throw them?"

"Honestly, it was Jody's idea and no, that's what the symbols are for. I was able to modify what I originally came up with so the magic will work with any user."

"Excellent. Jody's always got my back. That's why she's my first mate." I grab Cecily's hand and look toward the small boats. "It looks like our boat is ready. Let's go. I see Jody is already making her way to it. We better get there before she leaves us to swim to shore!"

Cecily laughs then nods as we make our way toward Jody and the small boat. She squeezes my hand as we walk the remainder of the way to our boat. I let Cecily step into the boat first and it wobbles beneath her, but she manages not to fall. I climb in after her and Jody smiles smugly at me. I roll my eyes in response and our boat begins to lower down into the water.

The small, mechanical joints creak as the rope moves through them above our heads. I look out at the water and see our crew making landfall before grabbing a set of oars. Jody grabs another set, and as soon as the boat is released atop the water, we begin to row.

I push my muscles as we move the boat forward across the waves, having not done it in quite some time. They feel heavy and underused. When I was a child Jody and I would row a small boat out into this bay to fish and I know from experience that my arms will be sore later.

I grunt as I fight against the waves and Cecily watches me intently. Her eyes sparkle with mirth as she remains seated between Jody and I. Glancing over Cecily's shoulder I catch Jody's eye and she sticks her tongue out at me. I guess she feels like her younger self being home again. It makes me chuckle and I find another bout of energy, which I thrust into rowing.

In what feels like hours later, we push our boat up on the sand. Jody and I pull it further up to keep it from washing back out into the bay after Cecily climbs out with Jody's aid, and we glance around.

My muscles burn but I ignore it as I observe the trees and sand before me. It's a bit overgrown but the remnants of old wooden stalls stick out from the sand. There was once a small market here and I would run up and down the beach while my father visited with each of them. It makes me sad to see coconuts scattered near where the baker's stall once stood. He would always have a treat for me and Jody.

I shake my head and pull myself back to the present. We've got a job to do. The crew stands casually watching me. They have eager looks on their faces and I bet they are as excited to be back as I am. I give them a nod and their smiles explode across their faces. They act like children as they take off at a sprint toward the old buildings laughing and cheering.

I laugh at their silliness and take a hold of Cecily's hand. I feel at ease being back on familiar ground. That sensation is short lived, though, as a scream fills the air and the Sparrow darts out from the trees with a small band of warriors.

"No!" I yell as adrenaline fills my veins. I drop Cecily's hand and reach for my sword. A hand on my shoulder stops me short.

"Take these instead!" She pushes a handful of vials into my hand.

I glance at the vials before meeting Cecily's gaze and nod. "Jody, keep her covered!" I meet my first mate's eyes and notice her sword is drawn.

"We'll be fine. Go, Silver." Jody places a hand on Cecily's shoulder and pulls her close.

I turn and sprint toward my men as the Sparrow's group engages them. She sees me and floats away enough to meet me head on.

I curse and grip the vials with one arm as I draw my sword. She has to make this difficult for me, doesn't she? Several of the vials slip from my hand as I near her and she gives it no mind. I raise my sword high as we meet, preparing to surprise her with the few remaining vials I have.

Our swords clash, jarring our arms with the force, and she uses her pixie flying ability to angle hers above me. I refuse to let it put me at a disadvantage and sidestep making her move. This causes her to turn, and we engage in a vicious onslaught. She seems faster than I remember, and more vials slip from my grip. There's no way I'll be able to throw one at her and keep her from skewering me!

"Give it up, Captain, and leave. This island is no longer your home." She sneers at me.

"It'll always be my home. You're the one that should be worried." I smile mischievously.

She engages me in our deadly dance with more vigor and I hold my ground. I parry each of her swings but as I attempt to sidestep to avoid her downward swing she surprises me by flipping a dagger out from her side. She thrusts it forward as I push weight into my foot to avoid it at the last minute and gets my arm. I cry out in pain, dropping the remaining vials, and whip my sword arm toward her in a vicious swing.

I hear shouts of surprise over my shoulder but refuse to move my focus away from my task. As the shouts increase, I struggle to keep my guard up, and ignore the fire in my arm. I can only hope the wound isn't deep. The Sparrow shoots up, surprising me, and stares off behind me.

"What's going on? What have you done?"

I allow myself to turn to figure out what she's staring at and see my crew gathered around several of the Sparrow's crew. They have them at sword point forcing them to kneel in a circle on the ground. A few other members of their crew hover in the air near the trees as if unsure of what to do. I start laughing as I see Cecily and Jody standing near the group with smug expressions on their faces.

"Find out and see." I wink at my girl, and watch as she tosses a vial as hard as she can toward us. It lands behind me and beneath the Sparrow before it explodes. Shimmering purple powder fills the air around me and a gentle breeze carries the scent of cinnamon through the air.

"What the hell?" She soars even higher, which moves her out of range from the dust. "You're using magic against me? How ridiculous. Two can play at that game."

I tilt my head sideways trying to understand her meaning and preparing for some sort of attack but instead, she zooms off leaving the few crew members we've captured behind. What kind of leader abandons her crew?

Sheathing my sword, I ignore the niggling doubt trying . to worm its way into my thoughts. I stride toward my crew as they stand proudly around their prey. Each continues to hold their swords toward the terror-stricken individuals.

"Great work everyone! Now, how about we get these lost

kids into town and take them to the old jail. Hopefully it's still standing."

"What have you done to us?" a boy with dirty blonde hair shouts, trying to move out of the sword circle.

"We took away your ability to use pixie dust," Cecily states for me proudly. "You'll never be able to use it again."

"What? How? Why?" a younger, mousy haired girl stutters out.

"We did it because your leader does not know when enough is enough. She's done terrorizing these waters. This island was once home to many magical creatures and people. Her family has run them off. No more. Her control ends." I place my hands on my hips and stare the kids down. "If you lot can prove yourself worthy, we'll let you have a peaceful life here in town. Wouldn't you like a warm bath?"

The mousy haired girl blinks at me as she processes my words. "Is that possible?"

I laugh as my palms sweat, does the heating magic still work here? "Yes. This town once had electricity and other fine things. We will share those with you if you'll cooperate."

"I'd love to have a warm bath, and clean clothes. What do I need to do to get that?" the girl asks eagerly.

Her response punches me in the gut, and I glance around at the kids. They're all ridiculously dirty and thin. What has been going on here? How did I not see it before? "Actually, we'll get you all fed first and go from there." I turn my gaze to my confused crew and see their faces soften into ones of concern and understanding. This isn't the first time we've stumbled our way into a situation like this. "Crew, get these kids into town and corralled in the jail. Once we get the food off loaded, we'll feed them and get things running again. Also, find a way to get that ship pulled up to shore. We're staying put for a while."

"Aye, aye, Captain." The crew gets to moving, pushing the kids toward the town, while two others step away and motion toward the ship.

"We're going to take care of them?" Jody asks incredulously, moving toward me with Cecily quietly at her side.

"Yes. I think they'll be more cooperative that way. Look at them, Jody. They're in terrible health."

She pauses and glances at the small group moving away from us. "I guess you're right. I've never paid that much attention to what they look like because they were trying to hack me to pieces with a sword."

"I've made them immune to pixie dust, so maybe that will cut down on their confidence with a sword. They won't be able to evade as easily," Cecily says softly. "Do you think the pixie dust had an impact on their health?" She steps closer and wraps me in her arms.

I frown watching the group get further away. "I don't know. I've never actually known anyone other than the Pan family who used it for a long period of time and they've always been off their rockers, so maybe?"

Cecily hums softly. "This might be something we should research. What if the pixie dust influences others outside the Pan line, but because the Pan family has something specific in their system, it only makes them go crazy instead of deteriorating their bodies?"

"Wow, Cecily, I'm impressed. That almost makes sense," Jody muses.

"Well, I guess we can work on finding out while here. Maybe it'll help us return the town to what it once was?"

Jody claps her hands together. "It's worth a shot!"

I nod in agreement but pause as the sound of a ticking clock fills the air. I meet Jody's wide-eyed gaze. "Is that..."

Chapter 10

I turn and stare at the water as blood pounds in my ears. Would we seriously have to fight off a crocodile now? First the Sparrow and her crew and now a giant ass croc?

A dark green head pops out of the water, its black eyes set on us. It swims in a zigzag pattern toward the shore. The animal appears larger than it was when I was a kid. Is that even possible? How is it even still alive?

The crocodile pulls itself further up the bank using its powerful legs as we stand frozen in place. Its massive body slides across the sand leaving a trail behind it as it goes. The sound of a ticking clock is louder now that it's out of the water and I stare at the face of a clock inlaid into its tail.

"That's the crocodile that took your dad and brother?" Cecily asks, jerking me out of my frozen state. She stands with her hands planted on her hips gazing at it calmly.

I grab her with my good arm and Jody snaps to her senses. Cecily stumbles as my weight pulls her into motion. "Yes, we need to run."

Cecily digs her feet into the sand fighting against my hold. It causes me to stumble so I meet her ferocious gaze.

Her face is determined, and her jaw is set. "No, he needs help. That's not a crocodile."

I pull on her harder. If we stay, I know it'll make a meal out of us. My palms sweat and I fight to ignore the pain from my wound. "It is too a crocodile! It's been pursuing my family for years!"

Cecily shakes her head and tosses one of the vials containing the potion at it. It breaks across the crocodile's head which causes a strange ripple of magic to move down its body. A loud pop followed by a blinding light causes my head to hurt and the ripples intensify across the animal staring at us.

"What the?" I gape, stunned.

"Watch," Cecily responds confidently. Her eyes fill with glee and a smile crosses her face and I glance between her and the crocodile.

The crocodile begins to change before my eyes. First its color changes from an inky green to a lighter tan color. Its stubby legs elongate and transition into arms and legs, human-looking ones. Seconds later it pushes up into standing and what was once a reptilian beast is now a man with shaggy black hair, grey eyes, and a rough beard.

"Holy shipwrecks. The crocodile's a human?" I gasp.

He blinks at me. "Of course I'm a human. I tried to find a way to convey that to you as a kid, but it didn't work. I was turned into this thing by the Pan family when I tried to take my child back from them many years ago. He's no longer living now. I watched him die at your father's hand."

"So, the Pans turned you?" Jody asks, moving closer to Cecily and me. "How did they use pixie dust to do that?"

"What? Pixie dust? Is that how it happened? I don't know how he did it, but they made me into that thing. What did you throw at me that helped me change back?" The man asks then glances down noticing his nudity for the first time. "I apologize, ladies, for my nudity. Could one of you give me your cloak to cover up?"

I shake my head, trying to process this strange situation. Never in a million years would I have imagined that the croc was once human.

I chuckle at how ludicrous this all is and pull off my leather overcoat before tossing it to him. He catches it easily and drapes it across his lower half, tying it at the waist. It does well to cover his midriff, but his long legs make it appear as if he has just slipped into a knee-length skirt.

"I tossed a potion that counteracts pixie dust at you. I could sense you weren't an animal," Cecily states as the man finishes tying the coat.

"How could you sense that? Are you a witch?" He tenses and his tan face pales.

"I guess you could call me that." She shrugs nonchalantly. "I know magic, but I'm not bad. Obviously." Cecily rolls her eyes.

"So, you've been stuck in that body for a long time then?" I switch our conversation away from giving people labels.

He nods. "I have. My name is Jaxon Ridge. I used to be a sailor."

"Well, we can at least put you to work. Do you know anything about where the Sparrow may be hiding?" I step forward to shake the man's hand. Urging this conversation forward and toward something that could benefit us all. I'm sure he's not a fan of the Sparrow considering the circumstances.

His grasp is firm and confident as he responds to the hand-shake. "I do. I can take you there. It's a simple ride up the river."

I smile eagerly as gears begin to churn in my head. The plan is changing but in a good way. "Let's get you into town and get clothes on you before we head to the hideout. We need to regroup and tend to some of those kids we saved from her earlier. They weren't in the best of shape, as I'm sure you've seen. Follow us."

With that, we all turn and head toward the ramshackle town. Jody hums a pleasant tune beside me as Cecily furrows her brow in thought. I wonder what she's thinking.

We walk as a group in silence for a time taking in the world around me. It's surreal to be back in the place I grew up but unnerving to see how much has been taken over by plants. Many buildings are now covered in vines and lay in pieces. Doors hang off hinges on a few and even fewer look livable. We'll have our hands full getting it back to something resembling what it once was.

"Jaxon," I ask, turning away from the overwhelming thoughts of repairing the town, "is it hard to get to where the hideout is?"

"No ma'am, it's not. It's right up the waterway there, maybe an hour or so of time in a boat. You follow the river into the mountain and then trek off into the trees a bit. The hideout used to be in the base of a tree, but the lady in charge has moved it into a cave."

I mull that over. "Do you know why she moved it?"

He shrugs. "I was never able to ask. She's a bit crazy, honestly. Her father was different. He had his wits about him but this new one, she's very off-kilter."

I nod and remain quiet. I don't want to kill her but if it came down to it, could I? How many people does she have trapped in that hideout? Is their condition as bad as those kids we captured today or worse?

Our group is quiet as we make our way further into town. I motion them forward to what used to be my home upon reaching the center of the small establishment. The fountain standing there marking the spot is dry but appears untouched. It's as if it's been preserved by magic. It gives me a surge of hope that we'll have hot water easier than I imagined. If the fountain is intact, all we have to do is add a bucket of water to activate it and it'll supply the entire area with fresh water.

Moving further down the lane, I see what's left of my family's old house. It's mostly in one piece with scorch marks across the left side of the house and rubble where my father's room once stood. The front steps look somewhat sturdy and without thought, I make my way up reaching to grab part of the rail only to pull my arm back in pain.

Glancing down, I stare at the wound from my fight with Sparrow and frown. Cecily gently grabs my arm and meets my gaze, eyes filled with concern. I let out a sigh as I look from her to the door. I gently pull it to me and glance at the buildings around me. So much to do and not enough time to get it done to keep us all safe. We'll have to manage as best as we can and act fast to get rid of the Sparrow. Maybe she'll be the only threat we face, at least for a time.

Squaring my shoulders I turn back to my friends and our new acquaintance. "Well this is home for a bit. Let's get in and see what we can scrounge up before heading over to check on the kids. Cecily, can you help me with my arm?"

"Yes, Silver, you know I will. Let's go see what we can find." She moves past me and pushes the door open.

Dust greets us as if it were a puff of smoke. Stale air and the smell of rotted wood moves with it.

"Hopefully we can find some candles as well, or something to help with the stale air. Ugh, in we go." I state and follow Cecily as she enters my childhood home wearing the expression of someone who's just discovered hidden treasure.

Chapter 11

I roll off the makeshift bed Cecily and I threw together before following over with sleep and stretch in the early light of dawn. The house is chilly since we left all the windows open to create a breeze. It smells much better after I found my family's old stash of incense and candles. A soft scent of mint lingers in the cool air as I move through my familiar routine to warm up my body.

Feeling better, I set out in search of my comrades only to find the house empty. How did they leave without waking me? Was that potion Cecily made for me stronger than I realized? I scratch my head while pursing my lips trying to recall what exactly the potion would do but my brain is still a bit foggy from having slept so hard.

Giving up, I head out of the house and back toward the center of town. I glance around as I walk thinking of the kids, we've now officially taken in. They eagerly accepted a position on my crew after their hot baths and the food we made them. The way they ate reminded me of leopards taking down prey, savage and fierce. How long had it been since they last ate enough to satisfy their hunger?

I sigh, shifting my thoughts to my wound and how it'll affect my ability to fight. I glance down at my arm hanging in my makeshift sling; can I take on the Sparrow one-handed if I need to? Could I attach a shield or something to it using rope? That would at least give me another way to defend myself. Maybe, Cecily has another potion that won't knock me on my ass, that'll increase the speed in which it heals?

I huff and glance at the building ahead of me. It's been a long time since I've seen it but it's impressive, nevertheless. My father built it with his bare hands, and he never mentioned that it had any spells cast on it, but with how it stands now, I think at one point, someone did place a protective spell or charm over it.

I enter the old building noticing that its brick walls have held well. My father believed that a strong town hall would help boost peoples' spirits and create a place of solidarity. It would also give us a place to discuss peace treaties and plan attacks if necessary. It's going to be used this morning for the latter.

I glance at the pictures that remain on the walls as I move across the entryway to a dusty hall filled with large wooden doors. Fresh candles burn brightly in their holders illuminating the dusty floor. The curtains sway in the light breeze coming through the window at the end of the hall. The old, cushioned bench I used to sit and read on while my father worked in his office rests beneath the window. It was the best place in this building to get fresh air and good light to dive into stories brought back from different countries by sailors who graced our shores.

I smile at the memory as I stop at the last door on the left side of the hall. My curiosity urges me to turn to the door behind me, hiding my father's office but alas, I have more important things to deal with than walking down memory lane right now. I need to discuss a plan of attack with my crew before exploring. The safety of my people here is more important and to guarantee that safety, I need to do something with the Sparrow.

With a deep breath, grab the brass knob and enter the old meeting room. I let the door swing closed behind me as I sweep the room with my eyes. I notice Jody hovering unusually close to Jaxon with a bright smile on her face. Her cheeks are a bit flushed, and her eyes look glazed over. Is she attracted to him? I've never seen her look at anyone like that. It might be good for her to have a significant other, even if said other was previously a crocodile and ate several of my family. It's not like he had much of a choice, right?

I shrug, pushing those thoughts to the back of my mind, and address the room. "Good morning, everyone. I see many of you have already met Jaxon. If not, everyone meet the previous croc of our nightmares."

My crew looks at Jaxon with raised brows before slowly edging away from him. Small bubble of space opens up around him except for my first mate still at his side.

He shrugs. "Yeah sorry about that. I didn't have much of a choice in that matter. That crazy Pan family had me under a spell."

I purse my lips and roll my eyes. "Any questions for him before we dive into planning?"

The room remains silent, but I catch a few people frowning and the occasional clenched fist. I guess they'll need time to adjust to this strange occurrence. I mean, Jaxon was the town's menace for years. The few on the crew who lived here at one point in time with family don't exactly share happy memories with his old form. Heck, I don't have good memories of his life as a crocodile, strange that it doesn't bother me more than it does, then again, William Pan was the one that pushed my father into the water atop his head.

I arch my brow as I look over each of my crew once again. "Well then, let's get started and take down the Sparrow. Jaxon, can you tell us more about her hideout? I know you mentioned briefly that it was up the river and in a cave, but are there any other specifics we should know about?"

He nods and steps forward, Jody oddly moving with him, then clears his throat. "Yes, the hideout is no longer in the base of a tree but in a large cave, as I told the Captain. She's forced the kids to excavate it and turn it into a system of tunnels for them to live in. The living conditions aren't great. They've been living there for several years and things have only gotten worse. The stench inside the cave is foul from sweat and the occasional animal carcass.

Many of them are afraid to leave for fear that the Sparrow will kill them. She summoned me to deal with one kid who refused to do her bidding, and well, you know what happens when she summons the crocodile."

Several grunts fill the room and I glance around, noticing a few nods and grimaces. Did the old Pan do this too or is this specific to the Sparrow? I can't recall if we ever kept track of their numbers in the past. Clearly we couldn't, being out on the water, but there only ever seemed to be a few familiar faces when she appeared. Hm.

I meet Jaxon's gaze offering him a nod of encouragement. He responds with a tight smile.

"Anyway, my memories as a crocodile are a bit jumbled up. So maybe the kid did something different that got him in trouble." He shrugs and bites his lip.

I glance over at Cecily. She watches Jaxon with her lips thinned. She had to make several healing spells and slaves last night for the kids. We found blankets in near perfect condition in a trunk at the old medical building for the kids to use. The crew even put together mattresses with fresh leaves from the forest so they could sleep on something soft. Some of them had thankful tears in their eyes as they curled up on them. They are all currently recovering in the old medical building's main floor space. I told them if they could help repair it, they could call it home until they were ready to build something new or head out to a new world.

Jaxon clears his throat once more and I focus again on the room around me.

"The only reason I was able to figure out how to get into the cave and see what they lived like was by sneaking in through a hollowed-out tunnel that connects to the river. I don't know if they meant to create the cavern it opens in, or if it was made naturally, but my croc form was able to swim in and meander through the hideout that way. It wasn't easy as there are some strange things on this island, but I remember the cave entrance well. If anyone came across me while I wandered, they ran the other way."

"Hmm, the cave seems like it would be an excellent access point to get in. How long did you stay beneath the surface to get into it?" Jody asks at his side before glancing at me. "That could be plan A."

I chuckle, which causes her to smile, before turning back to stare at her new obsession with starry eyes.

Several people fidget as the room grows quiet while Jaxon scratches his chin. The hair of his beard moving against his skin grates on my nerves, reminding me of sanding the deck as a child.

His eyes light up as he drops his hands and thankfully the repetitive, scratch, scratch, scratch stops. "I think about thirty minutes. I'm not sure because, as I mentioned, time was different in my other form. That stupid clock on my tail did nothing for me. I don't even know why it was placed there."

The room is silent, and no one fidgets, as I frown at Jaxon. The cave idea seems impossible. None of us can hold our breath for thirty minutes. We're not mermaids, or at least if one of the crew is, they haven't shared that. We'll have to go through the front if we can't get into the cave before drowning. It would be difficult to surprise them if we did that and it would guarantee deaths on both sides.

"I may have something that can help us with that," Cecily exclaims, springing from her chair and moving to her bag resting on an old table nearby. "I came across a spell that uses a certain plant to give the user gills. If you're all comfortable with that, we could use it to get in. It only lasts an hour and even above the water you'll be able to breathe normally."

I gape at her, utterly impressed at what magic can do. "How do we find this plant? Assuming there aren't any other ideas on how to get into the cave."

She pulls out a small bag from a pile at the table and digs around inside it. "Aha!" She holds a bottled item that looks like a giant wad of hair. "This is Tantula, it can be used in other spells, and I didn't realize until recently it could be used for underwater gills. Honestly, I thought it strange that it would be mentioned because who in their right mind would want gills, but here we are. Those of us who'll be entering through the cave will need to consume it brewed in tea. I suggest drinking it right before we plan to go under the water."

"Will it taste bad?" Jody crosses her arms with a frown, and I nod, having the same thought.

Cecily shrugs. "Probably but it's worth it right? It'll get us in and get the job done. Then we can focus on other things rather than dealing with the Sparrow, like what we're going to do with all of those she has with her. They're probably in similar shape to the kids we took in last night."

"That's a good point. I hadn't thought much past our plan of attack. If the others with her are interested, we can offer them a place to live here in town, if they help with repairs. Once we get the town back together then we can sail the seas again and have a place to return home to!" I smile, my heart feeling lighter. This will be our home again.

"Exactly!" she exclaims. "So, when do we want to get going and put our plan into action?"

"Slow down, I'm excited to get going too but we need to split up the crew. Jody, Jaxon and you have to go with me to the cave, but not all the crew do. We need volunteers to go with us and also to watch over the town. There are still other threats on this island and I'm sure they aren't the same kind we faced years ago." I turn and look at the members of my crew standing in the room.

"We should only need a few to go with us for the attack," Jody says, counting on her fingers. "Five should do it!"

"Yes, so, who volunteers?" I glance at the crew as Jody holds up five fingers eagerly in the air, wiggling them as she did as a kid.

The men and women grimace, throwing each other defeated looks, and I see they're concerned about this plan of attack. I mean will the gill's potion even work? It seems insane but magic tends to make anything sound crazy. We have to at least try this before we attack head on.

After a few minutes of me twiddling my thumbs and the crew whispering between themselves, five members stepped forward. Each has a determined look on their face and meets my steady gaze.

"Thanks." I let my eyes move to Cecily, who's busy cutting the hair-like plant into pieces. "Everything will work in our favor;

I have a feeling. Okay, the rest of you guard the town and continue to work on repairs. Cecily, get that tea ready and the rest of us will gather weapons. Jody, grab your stuff and get two boats ready. We'll paddle upriver and let Jaxon show us where we need to be. If the potion fails, we'll regroup and prepare for a full on frontal attack at the mouth of the cave. We'll all need to be there if plan B happens. We won't have the upper hand as we will with the surprise attack."

A resounding "Aye, aye, Captain!" fills the room as my crew burst into motion. The rustle of fabric and the murmuring of voices surrounds me as I move toward my father's old map hanging on the wall at the head of the room. It shows the waters and the few islands closest to Neverland.

Placing my hand on the green area titled Neverland, the busy room fades to nothing around me as I close my eyes and whisper to myself, "The Sparrow's reign ends today. I'm reclaiming you as my home and taking back the glory my family once had."

I keep my eyes closed for several minutes listening to my heart beat steadily. A tingling sensation spirals up my arm and I feel that I've been given a sign from the gods that my words have been heard. One way or another, this Island will be mine again.

Chapter 12

Water splashes noisily at the sides of the wooden boat as we make our way up the river. An occasional spray hits my knees sending a shocking jolt of cold through me but like my comrades, I remain quiet. I eagerly watch Jaxon seated at the head of our boat as he scans the water; my ears open waiting to hear that we've been spotted. We're unprotected in the open water, and the Sparrow could easily pick us off if she wanted. It leaves me feeling uneasy.

After what seems like an hour, feeling weary from being on high alert and with jugs of tea made, we make our way around a large bend. Vines hang down from the trees and we do our best to move them to the side as we move to the riverbank. The rushing sound of water moving through rapids further up from us provides a cover for the occasional groan coming from our boats.

I noticed Jaxon tense earlier and assumed we were close, and it took only a small hand gesture to move everyone out of the center of the river. Now I feel the heavy weight of everyone's gaze on my shoulders as I continue to watch Jaxon as he stares into the water.

Jaxon holds a hand over his brow as his eyes move side to side, looking for the entrance to the cave. Once we've reached the bottom of the cliff, hanging out over the bend, he holds his hand up.

"That's it, Captain." He rasps and points with a shaky hand toward a section of the cliff wall. Below it spins a small whirlpool.

"All right, group, let's get as close to that as possible without letting the boats get sucked in." I clear my throat having not spoken for some time and shake my shoulders in an attempt to loosen them up.

I hear light plops that seem to echo beneath the cliff as weights drop down into the water to keep our boats in place. They may not touch the bottom but will keep the boats from drifting.

Steadying myself as I stand, I reach out with my uninjured arm to grab the container of tea and take my part before passing it to my crew. The liquid slides down my throat and feels like I've swallowed an oversized spoonful of honey. It burns as it moves and I scratch at my neck as it warms. I fight the urge to dig into my skin as it begins to sting, clenching my fists at my side. Adrenaline kicks in as I wonder if the potion is giving me gills or if something else is happening. What if it kills us?

Slightly panicked, I glance around me as the rest of my crew takes their tea as if drinking shots of rum. As I meet Cecily's water gaze it feels like fire forces its way up my esophagus and my body breaks out in a cold sweat. I slam my eyes closed and cry out as sharp pain races across my throat then subsides. What just happened?

Confused, I blink, attempting to clear tears from my eyes and glance at Cecily. "Was there any description with that spell about pain?"

She shrugs before patting her neck. "It mentioned mild pain but that was more than mild. You okay?"

I let out a sigh, "I may be traumatized somewhat but I think I'll manage." I look at my weary-eyed crew. "You lot okay?"

They nod in response and several tenderly feel their necks. I look at Jody, who appears slightly pale but smiles trying to reassure me that she'll be okay.

"I guess it's into the water we go. Make sure your weapons are secure." I tighten my belt and check the knot holding my sword in place. I don't need to lose this in the water. I also grab the small bag holding the pixie neutralizer. It's sealed tight in a waterproof container and ready to go.

Standing from my seat, I look around at my crew as they wait for my signal. It's now or never. I turn facing the water and close my mouth tight. Hopefully, these gills work. I jump, well dive really, headfirst into the water causing the boat to rock behind me.

The chill of the water greets me as I sink down below the surface and open my eyes. I glance around and feel my gills moving slightly. I relax my jaw and smile as I feel as if I'm breathing normal air. Light filters down through the water creating a magical aquatic escape. Plants dance in the current and fish swim by. I would love to sit and take it all in, but I know that time is not on my side now. We have a task to complete.

Cecily, Jody, Jaxon, and the crew soon break through the surface and join me in the depths. Jody smiles like a child as she takes in the world around us and Cecily beams.

Jaxon motions toward me and I look at the vortex coming from the surface. Behind it rests the opening he mentioned that will lead us into the cave. How are we to get past the whirlpool though? That thing could suck us in, spit us out, and possibly cause some damage.

I watch, astonished, as Jaxon swims toward it confidently and grabs a large rock. He moves it over and as soon as he sets it down, the vortex disappears. I swim closer, curious, and notice another stone resting under it. Lifting the large one brings the whirlpool back, but it does nothing to me. It's an illusion!

Jaxon taps me on the arm before motioning me to follow. He swims into the pitch-black cave and I lose sight of him for a moment before something begins to glow. He pops out holding a strange eel that glows bright green and motions me forward. Here goes nothing!

I swim into the mouth of the cave following Jaxon and the glowing eel. Moving further in reveals a small group of the strange creatures who swarm us as they see their fellow eel. Their slimy bodies dance around us in greeting and I'm thankful they're friendly. They resemble electric eels quite a bit and I know those are dangerous.

The eels swim and dance around the crew and me as we continue forward. Their small wiggling bodies create a small current and they playfully swim around us. Did Jaxon interact with these little guys while still a crocodile? Is that why they're so gentle? I mean, we're invading their home and they're doing nothing to us.

I laugh causing a rush of bubbles to leave my mouth as two of the eels begin chasing each other around my arms as I swim. They try to catch the other's tail but move fast enough to stay out of reach. Soon they swim to my right and dart behind me, leaving me to follow Jaxon's lean form ahead of me.

I push my curious thoughts about the eels aside as the walls around us narrow. We're swimming in a tight space, and I'm forced to focus on the water passing through my gills as my claustrophobia rears its head. Now would be a terrible time to have a panic attack.

Thankfully, Jaxon breaks through the surface a few minutes later and pulls himself from the water. I wipe my eyes as my head clears the water seconds after him and take in the small tunnel and low rocky roof. There isn't a lot of room, so I must maneuver myself out of the water and down the tunnel slightly to allow my crew room to climb out. The only light in the cavern comes from the eels in the pool and a small glow from further into the cave. That must be where the hideout is.

Once clear of the water, everyone checks their weapons and I walk over to Cecily. She has a determined look on her face, but something seems to bother her. Her jaw has a twitch that I've never seen before.

"Hey, are you okay?" I gently grab her hand and rub calming circles with my thumb against her palm.

She gives me a pert nod. "Yes. The tight spaces on the way in messed with me. You?"

I smile and nod. "Same. I'm glad we won't be leaving the

same way. Are you ready for this?"

"I am. Let's go put a stop to this crazy lady."

"I like your spirit." I glance around at the crew. "Let's finish this once and for all. Jaxon, lead us there."

Everyone wipes what mud they can from their clothes grumbling as they do. I turn from them as they continue to fuss and stare at the pass ahead as my heart rate picks up. This is finally it, time to face my nemesis. I'll end her reign of chaos and free this island from her presence once and for all and Cecily and I will be able to live an easy life together.

Chapter 13

The cave swallows us with its stone walls as we move away from the watery entrance and the tunnel grows narrow. I take in the various bugs crawling in and out of its pock-marked surface as we move hoping one doesn't leap from the wall to my shoulder. I wince as bits of gravel fall nearby and glance around warily. Is this place stable? Will we need to dig our way out of here after facing the Sparrow instead of walking out?

Soon our path changes to one that's beaten down and I notice pallets roughly thrown together as we enter a larger part of the tunnel. The light is much brighter here with torches lining the walls. They aren't huge but the light is welcome, and the air is warmer. I swipe at the goosebumps on my skin as my body attempts to adjust, leading our party ever forward.

Looking around, muttering to myself at the pile of dirty blankets and clothes haphazardly strewn about, I scrunch my nose up. There is a smell lingering in the air that's a mix of feces and body odor. I try to hold my breath as we walk quietly but realize how stupid my idea is. There is no avoiding it this far in.

Voices filter from another entrance across the way and I hold my hand up, causing our party to pause. "We've got to get out of here. She's lost it. I can't believe she let them take the others! They could be dead now!"

"Calm down, Sadie. We'll find a way to get them back." A male's voice sounds defiant but doubtful.

"Should we dust them?" I jump as Cecily whispers close to my ear. I didn't hear her sneak up on me.

"That may be a good idea. They don't sound happy with their current situation, but one can never be too safe right?" I offer a small shrug and smile.

"Right, okay." She slips past me as if gliding on air and quietly moves around the corner. Her stealth is impressive, and I can't help but wonder if she's using some type of charm to aid her.

I shake my head to keep my thoughts from wandering down the rabbit hole and follow close to make sure no one attacks her. I draw my sword slowly to prevent any noise and hold it at the ready. Cecily pauses and I hold my breath as she grabs two vials out of her pouch and, quick as lightning, tosses them. I hear the shattering of glass as a shrill yelp fills the cavern.

Moving around the corner, I see two individuals staring at us, stunned. The female has poorly chopped hair and grime all over her clothes. The male looks even worse. Both have threadbare clothing draped across their bodies that barely covers them.

The male clears his throat. "How did you get in here?"

I step in front of Cecily, squaring my shoulders. "Why does it matter. I overheard your little discussion. Your friends are safe, not dead." Their shoulders drop and the girl purses her lips.

"You promise they're okay?" she asks, lifting her brow and crossing her arms.

I nod my head. "Yes, in fact they have access to clean water, clothes, and good food. Would you like to join them?"

"How? We can't just walk out of here. She won't let us." She looks over her shoulder as if the Sparrow might materialize from the walls.

"Leave that to us. Just get behind us or you can run ahead and share the news. We're putting an end to all this madness today."

"Okay, we'll follow you and give the others the hand sign that all is safe. I think we're all ready to be away from here anyway," the man says before grabbing the girl's hand and leading her to the back of our group.

"Alright, be ready, crew. Let's do this." The sound of swords being drawn echoes around me, and we set out to look for the Sparrow.

Shouts fill the air as we enter another large cavern and I press my lips together to keep my emotions in check as our new friends share their hand signals and each face around the room turns to confusion. Before long a crowd grows behind us as we move through more and more tunnels. We're no longer silent as we move but with as many people following, there shouldn't be many to fight upon finding the Sparrow.

"Where can she be?" I mumble aloud and then stop as we round a tight corner and discover the mouth of the cave. The wide entrance opens to the jungle-like forest and green plants sway in the breeze. There leaning against the inside wall glaring at me is the Sparrow, a knowing look on her face, and hand resting on the pommel of her sword.

"How dare you enter my home!" She pushes away from the wall and draws her sword. That moment is all we need and the look in her eyes widens as a glass vial shatters against her face.

I hold back my laugh as the powder drips from her face but her stunned expression changes rapidly from surprise to rage. She launches herself forward toward me, stumbling slightly, having lost her ability to fly. She's no longer used to fighting on the ground, which gives me an advantage. I meet her head on and our swords clash echoing around the cave.

"Get everyone out, Jody!" I yell using my one good arm to face off against my nemesis.

"No! You'll not take them! They're mine! They can never leave!" she yells, spittle flying from her mouth and landing on my face. She's out of her mind and reminds me of a rabid dog foaming at the mouth.

"People are not keepsakes! Have you lost your mind?

They're in terrible shape. You're killing them by keeping them here!" I grunt as I push against her sword. She stumbles back, fighting to keep her balance, but regroups quickly, and comes at me again.

She puts more power behind her thrusts as she screams, making me wince. Does she not want to admit that she's doing more harm than good? Her family didn't start out like this. When did the corruption set in? Was it really the pixie dust? Her reaction only leaves me with one choice. I don't want to do it, but it must be done. She's beyond reasoning with and the neutralizing dust can only do so much.

Feeling sweat on my brow and down my back, I dread what I must do next as we continue to spin in this deadly dance. My good arm aches as I struggle to fight her off and get an opening on her. She spins and hits my damaged arm with an elbow before aiming for my face but I manage to lean my head to the side letting her elbow swing by.

The move causes her to stagger, and she takes a moment to regroup. Seeing my opening, I sidestep to the left as the Sparrow swings her sword up in an arc. I drop low, keeping my sore arm out of range, and slice up and across, catching her torso. The hit is dead on, and I feel the contact of the sword against her flesh as it vibrates down my hilt.

She drops her sword and falls into a heap, tears streaming down her face. My heart aches but I know what must be done. Her reign cannot go on any longer. This is a mercy for her, one that I wish needn't be done, but this insanity can't continue. Peoples' lives are at stake and it's time for me and mine to come home.

With tears streaming from my own eyes, I meet her gaze. "I can give you a second chance, Norma, but this madness must stop. You can't control this island anymore. Let us try to help you."

"No! You're people don't belong here! They're filth." She spits and I don't miss the tinge of blood in it. "My family wanted to make this place a kingdom and take in those lost kids. I've rescued every one of mine from the streets of different worlds. What could you give us that I can't?" She tries to push from the ground holding her side with one arm.

I shake my head. "Do you not see what state they are in? This isn't healthy!"

She bares her teeth once again filling my mind's eye with an image of an animal possessed. "I will never give in."

I close my eyes and take a breath to prepare myself as I lift my sword high. Opening my eyes, I meet her gaze, and steady my arm. "Then I have no other choice," the words come out in a whisper, and I bring my sword down, removing her head from her body. I stare for a moment as it rolls gently a foot or two away before dropping to my knees.

If my brother and his wife ever find out, will they forgive me? It's one thing to end a life, but this? Did I make the right choice? Should I have tried to force her to try and see reason?

A hand rests on my shoulder. "You did the right thing, Silver. Everyone is out. Let's go."

I glance up at Cecily and nod. Wordlessly I push myself up and she grabs my hand. She leads me out of the cave, and we remain holding hands until we get back to the small village. It's all over, finally over. We rescued those she had trapped but now I must deal with the guilt of ending her life and facing my sister-in-law in the future. Will she hold this against me or understand the need for my choice? Will the Sparrows end forever haunt me?

Chapter 14

Once back in the old town, I let Cecily lead me to our new home. None of the others follow us and I assume she talked with them beforehand. The extra space and quiet is something I need while I try to process.

"Jody is going to handle the new refugees we brought back with us. How about we make you some tea and get you in a warm bath?" She guides me into the house and down the hall where one of the few bathrooms is. We managed to wrangle up some towels when we arrived that weren't in terrible condition and had soap brought over from the ship after we decided to help the kids.

I watch her silently as she runs the water letting my emotions spiral in my mind. The Pan family has been around since before I was born and now, I've brought an end to them. Yes, I'm free to pirate and do as I please but it feels like the end of an era. My family can finally return home if they want, and pirates can once again live in our town, but guilt hovers like a dark cloud over me and I don't understand why there is so much of it. Could it be the fear of what my sister-in-law will think or is there more? It doesn't make sense.

"Are you okay?" Cecily snaps her fingers in front of my face, getting my attention. "I've asked you several questions and you didn't even flinch."

I shake my head trying to clear it. "It's a lot to take in. I will be in time. Are you sure we got everyone out?"

"We did. It's over and now we can finally spend some time together without making spells or coming up with a plan to get rid of the Sparrow. She's officially gone." Cecily reaches forward and pulls at my top. Her gaze is heated, and I know what she wants.

She pulls it over my head, and I smile at her softly. "I guess that's one way to look at it. So, you're really going to stay with me?"

Cecily laughs and moves to straddle me. She pulls my face into her hands. "Of course, I'm staying with you Silver. You've changed my life. I think too that this small town could use someone with magic skills. I do know many healing spells after all. Who do you think took care of my grandmother? Besides, look at all the people we saved."

I laugh wrapping my arms around her waist. "I didn't think about that. You know you're getting blood all over you?"

"Eh, it's only a little. The worst part of it was on your shirt, which is gone. I may need to burn it because I don't think we can get all that blood out. Now let's get into this water and enjoy ourselves. Once you're feeling better, you have a town to finish organizing and people to lead. Even if you sail the world, are gone a lot, whatever, these people are going to look to you to lead them. Now, you silly captain, let's celebrate our new life. Together forever."

"Alright there, sassy pants, whatever you say. Together forever. I like the sound of that."

I stand still holding her and move us closer to the tub. Stopping, she slowly lowers her legs to the ground. We finish undressing and ease into the water, still holding hands. I've never had much of a relaxing life. I've always been on my guard watching for attackers. Now though, I think I can finally let go of some stress and live a more carefree life. I feel like anything is possible if I have Cecily by my side.

I watch as Cecily eases into the water ahead of me and steam surrounds her. This woman helped me find my freedom from the Sparrow. I hope that in return, I can give her the life she deserves, free of poverty and fear. We'll be happy and when we're ready, we'll marry.

So many possibilities dance in my mind as I join her in the warm water. So many open doors now sit in front of me. First, I'll rebuild this town and get it established. So many here need to know this peace, and maybe, just maybe, I can bring my brother home. Then, with Cecily as my wife, we can sail the seas and help those women who need us while also pirating from the greedy to help our community. No better way to be a pirate, right?

Epilogue

6 months later...

The cool breeze pushes my hair out of my face as I stand at the helm of my ship staring at Neverland on the horizon. I sent a message to my brother shortly after defeating the Sparrow and now he and his family of six rest in my cabin ready to return to the family home. Jody remained at the island with Cecily while I went to retrieve my family at the Mermaid's Portal in Xandu.

My sister-in-law was sad at the news of her sister's death but also understanding. She claimed she had issues adjusting to being away from the dust and went through a long period of withdrawal before her body finally returned to normal. It reaffirmed my thought on how the dust affected the Sparrow.

Now I fight the tears trying to escape my eyes as my ship sails closer. Being away from my love has been torture and I can't wait to hold her once again. Four months at sea without her was too long.

Soon, we near the long dock we rebuilt into the new harbor. A small party stands on it, waving wildly at us. Looking closer I notice something about Jody is different. Squinting my eyes, since we aren't quite close enough to speak, I see her middle is rounder.

"What the—"

"Is that Jody?"

I turn as my brother, Roger, steps to my side. His long dark hair falls in small braids around his head. A string of beads covers one of the braids next to his left temple. "Yes, it is, or at least I think it is."

"You didn't tell me she was pregnant." He arches his brow and tilts his head.

"It's news to me too. I guess she got serious with someone while I was away." I stare back out across the water, placing my hands on my hips.

His deep baritone chuckle dances through the air around

me. "Well, I guess we'll find out what happened soon enough."

I snort and shake my head. "I guess we will."

The End

Maps and Other Images

Parts of a Ship

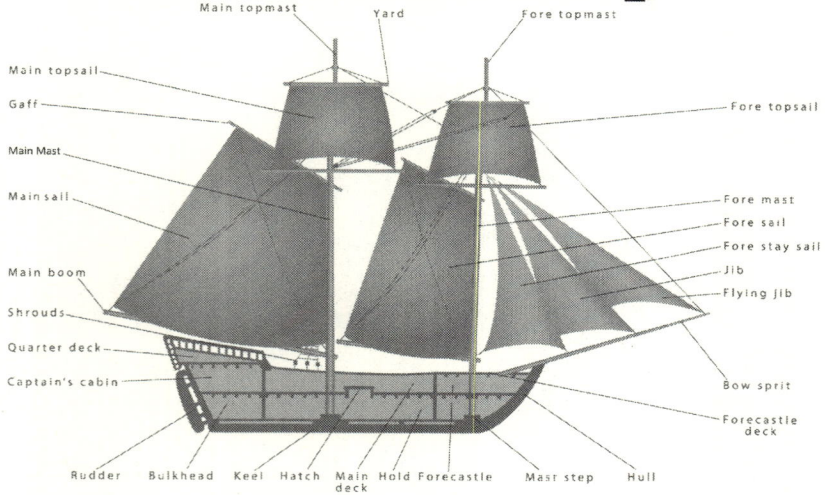

Main topmast — Yard — Fore topmast

Main topsail
Gaff
Main Mast
Main sail
Main boom
Shrouds
Quarter deck
Captain's cabin

Fore topsail
Fore mast
Fore sail
Fore stay sail
Jib
Flying jib

Bow sprit
Forecastle deck

Rudder   Bulkhead   Keel   Hatch   Main deck   Hold   Forecastle   Mast step   Hull

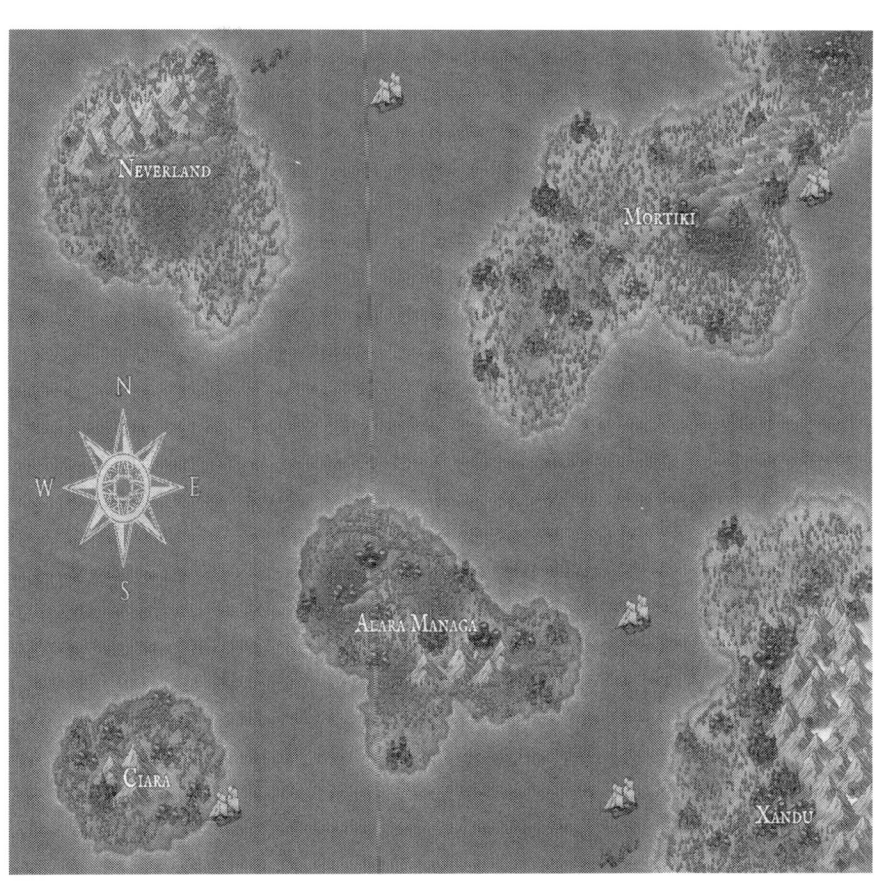

Hooked Playlist

- Skull and Bones by Home Free

- Wellerman- Sea Shanty by Nathan Evans

- Song of the Vikings (My Mother Told Me) by Perly I Lotry

- Brisbane Harbour by The Dreadnoughts

- Look What You Made Me Do by Taylor Swift

- Anti-Hero by Taylor Swift

- The Better Me by Beartooth, HARDY

- I'll Make a Man Out of You by Peyton Parrish

- Drunken Sailor by MALINDA, Bobby Bass, Mia Asano, Piper.Ally, Cullen Vance, and Seth Staton Watkins

- Ragnarök by Peyton Parrish

- Go the Distance by Peyton Parrish

Acknowledgements

I have so many people to thank for this story! First, I want to thank you, the reader, for reaching this point. I would love to hear your thoughts on this story. Please drop a review on the platform you purchased this book from and share it on social media. Be sure to either tag me or use #MadilynnDale #Hooked #TheChaptergoddess.

I want to thank next my Beta readers, ARC readers, and my fantastic editor Lily Luchesi. Also, my family and friends offering support as this story came to fruition. This includes those in The Writing Tribe, Go Indie Now, and others across the world.

The biggest thank you goes to my husband and my son for letting me pursue my dream as an author. Your love and support has been the backbone of my ability to keep going. Thank you both for being my rock.

About The Author

Madilynn Dale is an author, blogger, freelancer, podcaster, producer, reader, mother, author coach, ghostwriter, proofreader, and overall creative. She's a host for several shows featured under the Go Indie Now's wide umbrella, hosts a podcast channel of her own, The Chapter Goddess Chat, and loves to travel. Madilynn enjoys chatting with creatives from all areas of the field and letting her viewers see the authentic side of each one of them.

Madilynn is an Oklahoma author and holds several different degrees. She has a bachelor's degree in Kinesiology and an associate degree in Physical Therapy Assistant Sciences. Her creativity stems from something deep within, and through her bond with the creative flow, brings her stories to life. She never envisioned herself as a writer but took a leap of faith while pregnant and began a new journey. She enjoyed writing short stories as a kid and has been an avid reader since grade school.

Madilynn's hobbies, when not writing, include reading, baking, crafting, hiking, playing with her son, caring for her rescue pets, gardening, teaching, and horseback riding. She loves to travel and explore. One day she hopes to expand her travels and see the world, but in the meantime, you'll find her working on her next novel.

https://www.thechaptergoddess.com/

Made in the USA
Columbia, SC
03 June 2024

36229942R00052